EVERYDAY Literacy
Science

GRADE
1

Download Home–School Activities in Spanish

The Home–School Connection at the end of each weekly lesson in the book is also available in Spanish on our website.

How to Download:

1. Go to www.evan-moor.com/resources.

2. Enter your e-mail address and the resource code for this product—EMC5026.

3. You will receive an e-mail with a link to the downloadable letters, as well as an attachment with instructions.

Writing: Barbara Allman
Content Editing: Guadalupe Lopez
Lisa Vitarisi Mathews
Andrea Weiss
Copy Editing: Cathy Harber
Art Direction: Cheryl Puckett
Kathy Kopp
Cover Design: Cheryl Puckett
Illustrator: Mary Rojas
Design/Production: Carolina Caird

EMC 5026

Evan-Moor®
EDUCATIONAL PUBLISHERS
Helping Children Learn since 1979

Visit
teaching-standards.com
to view a correlation
of this book.
This is a free service.

Correlated to State and Common Core State Standards

Congratulations on your purchase of some of the finest teaching materials in the world.

Contents

What's Inside

In this book, you will find **20 weekly lessons**. Each weekly lesson includes:

3 Teacher Pages

Use these pages to guide you through the week.

A script to follow that introduces the science concept

A short story to read aloud to students

Daily discussion questions about the story or science concept, plus a script to guide students through the activities

A hands-on activity that reinforces the weekly concept

Sample of students' expected responses

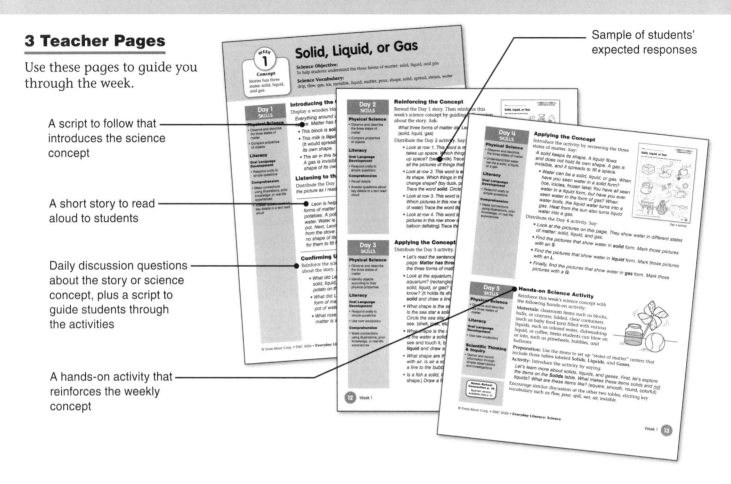

4 Student Activity Pages

Reproduce each page for students to complete during the daily lesson.

1 Home–School Connection Page

At the end of each week, give students the **Home–School Connection** page (in English or Spanish) to take home and share with their parents.

To access the Spanish version of the activity, go to www.evan-moor.com/resources. Enter your e-mail address and the resource code EMC5026.

Everyday Literacy: Science • EMC 5026 • © Evan-Moor Corp.

How to Use This Book

Follow these easy steps to conduct the lessons:

Day 1

Reproduce and distribute the *Day 1 Student Page* to each student.

Use the scripted *Day 1 Teacher Page* to:

1. Introduce the weekly concept.

2. Read the story aloud as students listen and look at the picture.

3. Guide students through the activity.

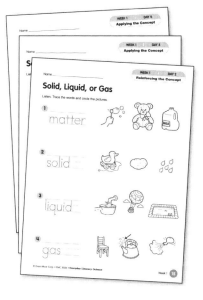

Days 2, 3, and 4

Reproduce and distribute the appropriate day's activity page to each student.

Use the scripted *Teacher Page* to:

1. Review and discuss the Day 1 story.

2. Reinforce, develop, apply, or extend the science concept.

3. Guide students through the activity.

Home–School Connection

Day 5

Follow the directions to lead the Hands-on Science Activity.

Send home the **Home–School Connection** page for each student to complete with his or her parents.

Tips for Success

- Review the *Teacher Page* before you begin the lesson.

- Work with students in small groups at a table in a quiet area of the room.

- Model how to respond to questions by using complete sentences. For example, if a student responds to the question "Where does rain come from?" by answering "clouds," you'd respond, "That's right. Rain comes from the clouds."

- Wait for students to complete each task before giving the next direction.

- Provide visual aids or concrete demonstrations when possible.

Skills Chart

Week	Observe and describe the three states of matter	Identify objects according to their physical properties	Understand that water can be a solid, a liquid, or a gas	Understand the different ways that water behaves	Understand that properties of solids can change when mixed, cooled, or heated	Understand that systems have parts	Identify parts that, when put together, can do things they cannot do by themselves	Understand that people, plants, and animals are living things with basic needs	Understand that animals inhabit many different places	Identify ways in which an animal's habitat provides for its basic needs	Identify and describe the parts of a plant	Infer what animals eat from the shapes of their teeth	Understand that green leaves make food from sunlight	Understand that leaves have parts	Recognize that animals have life cycles	Understand that living things grow and change	Recognize changes in appearance that animals go through as seasons change	Understand that some animal behaviors are influenced by environmental conditions	Describe ways in which animals closely resemble their parents in appearance	Understand that people are living things that have parts	Identify the functions of the physical structures of insects	Recognize that water, rocks, soil, and living organisms are found on Earth's surface
	Physical Science							Life Science														
1	•	•	•																			
2					•																	
3	•			•																		
4		•	•																			
5						•	•															
6																						
7								•	•	•												
8											•											
9								•				•										
10								•					•	•								
11								•							•	•						
12								•									•	•				
13																•			•			
14																				•		
15								•														
16																					•	
17																						•
18																						•
19																						
20																						

Everyday Literacy: Science • EMC 5026 • © Evan-Moor Corp.

Earth Science					Scientific Thinking & Inquiry						Investigation		Oral Language Development				Comprehension				
Observe and describe differences in rocks	Identify a variety of natural sources of water	Understand that weather can be observed and measured using simple tools	Understand that weather changes across days and seasons	Understand that the sun supplies heat and light and is necessary for life	Predict, observe, and examine different substances to determine their ability to mix with water	Sort objects according to common characteristics	Design a simple system	Manipulate a system so that when a part is separated from the whole, the system fails	Gather and record information through simple observations and investigations	Interpret information found in charts	Identify objects that create specific sounds	Understand how sound is made	Name and describe pictured objects	Respond orally to simple questions	Use traditional structures, such as cause and effect, to convey information	Use new vocabulary	Recall details	Make connections using illustrations, prior knowledge, or real-life experiences	Answer questions about key details in a text read aloud	Make inferences and draw conclusions	Week
									•					•		•	•	•	•		1
									•				•	•	•	•	•	•	•		2
		•			•				•				•	•		•	•	•	•		3
									•					•		•	•	•	•		4
							•	•					•	•		•	•	•	•		5
									•		•	•		•		•	•	•	•	•	6
														•		•	•	•	•	•	7
						•			•	•				•		•	•	•	•	•	8
									•					•		•	•	•	•	•	9
									•					•		•	•	•	•	•	10
														•		•	•	•	•	•	11
						•								•		•	•	•	•	•	12
														•		•	•	•	•	•	13
														•		•	•	•	•	•	14
						•								•		•	•	•	•	•	15
														•		•	•	•	•		16
•									•					•		•	•	•	•	•	17
	•													•		•	•	•	•	•	18
		•	•						•	•				•		•	•	•	•	•	19
				•					•	•			•	•	•	•	•	•	•	•	20

Everyday Literacy
Science

Student Progress Record

Name: _____

Write dates and comments in the boxes
below the student's proficiency level.

1: Rarely demonstrates   0 – 25 %
2: Occasionally demonstrates   25 – 50 %
3: Usually demonstrates   50 – 75 %
4: Consistently demonstrates   75 – 100 %

Literacy Skills	1	2	3	4
Forms letters legibly				
Tracks print and pictures from top to bottom and left to right				
Writes words from a word box				

Oral Language Development

Uses descriptive language				
Names and describes pictured objects				
Responds orally to simple questions				

Comprehension

Recalls details				
Makes connections using illustrations, prior knowledge, or real-life experiences				
Makes inferences and draws conclusions				

Science

Uses content vocabulary when speaking				
Engages in scientific thinking and inquiry				

Everyday Literacy
Science

Students' Names:

Small-Group Record Sheet

Write dates and comments about students' performance each week.

Week	Title	Comments
1	Solid, Liquid, or Gas	
2	Looking at Solids	
3	Looking at Liquids	
4	Where Is the Water?	
5	Parts Work Together	
6	Making Sound	
7	Where Animals Live	
8	Plants Are Food	
9	What Do Animals Eat?	
10	Looking at Leaves	
11	Growing and Changing	
12	Animals in Winter	
13	Animals and Their Babies	
14	The Brain and Skull	
15	Food for Energy	
16	Parts of an Insect	
17	Looking at Rocks	
18	Bodies of Water	
19	Recording the Weather	
20	Our Sun	

Dear Parent or Guardian,

Every week your child will learn a concept that focuses on Physical Science, Life Science, Earth Science, or Investigation. Your child will develop oral language and comprehension skills by listening to stories and engaging in oral, written, and hands-on activities that reinforce science concepts.

At the end of each week, I will send home an activity page for you to complete with your child. The activity page reviews the weekly science concept and has an activity for you and your child to do together.

Sincerely,

Estimado padre o tutor:

Cada semana su niño(a) aprenderá sobre un concepto de ciencias físicas, naturales, de la Tierra o sobre investigación. Su niño(a) desarrollará las habilidades de lenguaje oral y de comprensión escuchando cuentos y realizando actividades orales y escritas. Además, participará en actividades prácticas que apoyan los conceptos de ciencias.

Al final de cada semana, le enviaré una hoja de actividades para que la complete en casa con su niño(a). La hoja repasa el concepto científico de la semana, y contiene una actividad que pueden completar usted y su niño(a) juntos.

Atentamente,

Solid, Liquid, or Gas

Science Objective:
To help students understand the three forms of matter: solid, liquid, and gas

Science Vocabulary:
drip, flow, gas, ice, invisible, liquid, matter, pour, shape, solid, spread, steam, water

Day 1
SKILLS

Physical Science
- Observe and describe the three states of matter
- Compare properties of objects

Literacy

Oral Language Development
- Respond orally to simple questions

Comprehension
- Make connections using illustrations, prior knowledge, or real-life experiences
- Answer questions about key details in a text read aloud

Introducing the Concept

Display a wooden block, a carton of milk, and an inflated balloon. Say:

*Everything around us is called **matter**. Matter is anything that takes up space. Matter has three forms: solid, liquid, and gas.*

- *This block is **solid**. You can easily see a solid. A solid holds its shape.*
- *This milk is **liquid**. What would happen if the milk weren't in the carton? (It would spread out.) A liquid can flow, pour, or drip. It can <u>not</u> hold its own shape.*
- *The air in this balloon is a **gas**. The air that you breathe is also a gas. A gas is invisible; you can't see it, but it is still there. A gas has no shape of its own. It spreads out to fill a space.*

Listening to the Story

Distribute the Day 1 activity page to each student. Say: *Listen and look at the picture as I read a story about a boy who thinks about matter.*

Leon is helping his grandma prepare dinner. He notices the three forms of matter he learned about in school. First, he washes some potatoes. A potato is a solid. It holds its shape. Then Leon fills a pot with water. Water is a liquid. It pours out of the faucet. It takes the shape of the pot. Next, Leon's grandma heats the water to cook the potatoes. The heat from the stove slowly changes the liquid water into steam, a gas. It has no shape of its own. Leon is glad that potatoes are a solid. He can't wait for them to fill his tummy. Preparing dinner is making him hungry!

Confirming Understanding

Reinforce the science concept by asking questions about the story. Ask:

- *What did Leon wash? (potatoes) Are potatoes solid, liquid, or gas? (solid) Draw another potato on the counter.*
- *What did Leon fill the pot with? (water) What form of matter is water? (liquid) Underline the pot of water.*
- *What rose into the air? (steam) What form of matter is steam? (gas) Circle the steam.*

Day 1 picture

Physical Science

• Observe and describe the three states of matter

• Compare properties of objects

Literacy

Oral Language Development

• Respond orally to simple questions

Comprehension

• Recall details

• Answer questions about key details in a text read aloud

Reinforcing the Concept

Reread the Day 1 story. Then reinforce this week's science concept by guiding a discussion about the story. Ask:

What three forms of matter did Leon think about? (solid, liquid, gas)

Distribute the Day 2 activity. Say:

• *Look at row 1. This word is* **matter**. *Matter takes up space. Which things in this row take up space?* (bear, milk) *Trace the word. Circle all the pictures of things that are* **matter**.

• *Look at row 2. This word is* **solid**. *A solid holds its shape. Which things in this row do* <u>not</u> *change shape?* (toy duck, potato) *Trace the word* **solid**. *Circle the solids.*

• *Look at row 3. This word is* **liquid**. *A liquid takes the shape of its container. Which pictures in this row show a liquid in a container?* (pot of water, pool of water) *Trace the word* **liquid**. *Circle the liquids.*

• *Look at row 4. This word is* **gas**. *A gas spreads out to fill a space. Which pictures in this row show a gas spreading out?* (steam coming out of kettle; balloon deflating) *Trace the word* **gas**. *Circle the gases.*

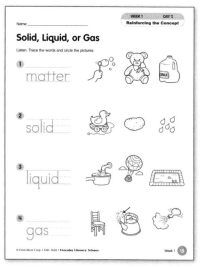

Day 2 activity

Physical Science

• Observe and describe the three states of matter

• Identify objects according to their physical properties

Literacy

Oral Language Development

• Respond orally to simple questions

• Use new vocabulary

Comprehension

• Make connections using illustrations, prior knowledge, or real-life experiences

Applying the Concept

Distribute the Day 3 activity. Say:

• *Let's read the sentence at the top of this page:* **Matter has three forms.** *What are the three forms of matter?* (solid, liquid, gas)

• *Look at the aquarium. What shape is the aquarium?* (rectangle) *Is the aquarium a solid, liquid, or gas?* (solid) *How do you know?* (It holds its shape.) *Trace the word* **solid** *and draw a line to the aquarium.*

• *What shape is the sea star?* (star-shaped) *Is the sea star a solid, liquid, or gas?* (solid) *Circle the sea star and any other solids you see.* (shell, rock, etc.)

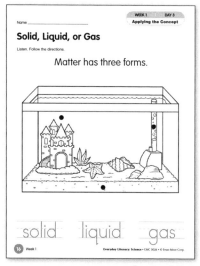

Day 3 activity

• *What shape is the water?* (same shape as the aquarium that holds it) *Is the water a solid, liquid, or gas?* (liquid) *How do you know?* (You can see and touch it, but it doesn't hold its own shape.) *Trace the word* **liquid** *and draw a line to the water.*

• *What shape are the bubbles in the filter?* (round) *The bubbles are filled with air. Is air a solid, liquid, or gas?* (gas) *Trace the word* **gas** *and draw a line to the bubbles.*

• *Is a fish a solid, liquid, or gas?* (solid) *How do you know?* (It holds its shape.) *Draw a fish in the aquarium.*

Physical Science
- Observe and describe the three states of matter
- Understand that water can be a solid, a liquid, or a gas

Literacy

Oral Language Development
- Respond orally to simple questions

Comprehension
- Make connections using illustrations, prior knowledge, or real-life experiences

Applying the Concept

Introduce the activity by reviewing the three states of matter. Say:

A solid keeps its shape. A liquid flows and does not hold its own shape. A gas is invisible, and it spreads to fill a space.

- *Water can be a solid, liquid, or gas. When have you seen water in a solid form?* (ice, icicles, frozen lake) *You have all seen water in a liquid form, but have you ever seen water in the form of gas? When water boils, the liquid water turns into a gas. Heat from the sun also turns liquid water into a gas.*

Day 4 activity

Distribute the Day 4 activity. Say:

- *Look at the pictures on this page. They show water in different states of matter: solid, liquid, and gas.*

- *Find the pictures that show water in **solid** form. Mark those pictures with an **S**.*

- *Find the pictures that show water in **liquid** form. Mark those pictures with an **L**.*

- *Finally, find the pictures that show water in **gas** form. Mark those pictures with a **G**.*

Physical Science
- Observe and describe the three states of matter

Literacy

Oral Language Development
- Use new vocabulary

Scientific Thinking & Inquiry
- Gather and record information through simple observations and investigations

Home–School Connection p. 18
Spanish version available (see p. 2)

Hands-on Science Activity

Reinforce this week's science concept with the following hands-on activity:

Materials: classroom items such as blocks, balls, or crayons; lidded, clear containers (such as baby food jars) filled with various liquids, such as colored water, dishwashing liquid, or coffee; items students can blow on or into, such as pinwheels, bubbles, and balloons

Preparation: Use the items to set up "states of matter" centers that include three tables labeled **Solids**, **Liquids**, and **Gases**.

Activity: Introduce the activity by saying:

*Let's learn more about solids, liquids, and gases. First, let's explore the items on the **Solids** table. What makes these items solids and not liquids? What are these items like?* (square, smooth, round, colorful)

Encourage similar discussion at the other two tables, eliciting key vocabulary such as *flow, pour, spill, wet, air, invisible.*

Name _____

Solid, Liquid, or Gas

Name _____

Solid, Liquid, or Gas

Listen. Trace the words and circle the pictures.

1 _____

matter

2 _____

solid

3 _____

liquid

  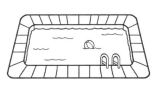

4 _____

gas

Name _____

Solid, Liquid, or Gas

Listen. Follow the directions.

Matter has three forms.

Everyday Literacy: Science • EMC 5026 • © Evan-Moor Corp.

Name _____

Solid, Liquid, or Gas

Listen. Mark the solids with an **S**, the liquids with an **L**, and the gases with a **G**.

Name _____

What I Learned

What to Do
Look at the picture below with your child. Name an object in the picture and have your child identify it as a *solid, liquid,* or *gas.* For example: potatoes, spoons (solid); water (liquid); and steam, air (gas).

Science Concept: Matter has three states: solid, liquid, and gas.

To Parents
This week your child learned that matter can be a solid, liquid, or gas.

What to Do Next
Give your child three sticky notes and have him or her write **solid**, **liquid**, or **gas** on each one. Then have your child place the notes around the house to label different objects.

Looking at Solids

Science Objective:
To help students understand that heat changes solids and that solids can be combined into mixtures

Science Vocabulary:
heat, liquid, matter, melt, mixture, solid

Day 1
SKILLS

Physical Science

• Understand that properties of solids can change when mixed, cooled, or heated

Literacy

Oral Language Development

• Name and describe pictured objects

• Respond orally to simple questions

• Use traditional structures, such as cause and effect, to convey information

Comprehension

• Make connections using illustrations, prior knowledge, or real-life experiences

• Answer questions about key details in a text read aloud

Introducing the Concept

Prepare for the lesson by gathering a variety of objects around the classroom that are solids. Point to each solid as you say:

• *A **solid** is matter that keeps its own shape. When a solid gets very hot, it can change into a liquid. When that happens, we say the solid **melts**. What happens to an ice cube if you put it in a warm place?* (It melts.)

• *What other solids have you seen melt?* (ice cream, snowman, candle, cheese) *What caused the solids to melt?* (the sun, heat, cooking)

Listening to the Story

Distribute the Day 1 activity page to each student. Say: *Listen and look at the picture as I read about students who are learning about solids.*

Mrs. Garcia's class is learning about matter. The children know that solids are a form of matter. Mrs. Garcia asked the children to name foods in their lunches that are solids. Colin said, "I have carrots. A carrot is a solid. It keeps its shape." Julia said, "I have cheese. Cheese is a solid." Tyler said, "I have a bread roll. A bread roll is a solid." Alita said, "I have a chocolate bar. It is a solid. But if you leave it in the car on a hot day, it will melt into a liquid. Thank goodness chocolate tastes great whether it's a solid or a liquid!"

Confirming Understanding

Reinforce the science concept by asking questions about the story. Ask:

• *Which solids did the children name?* (carrots, cheese, bread, chocolate) *Circle each of those solids.*

• *Which solid will melt if it is left in the car on a hot day?* (chocolate) *What will make it melt?* (heat) *Make an **X** on the chocolate bar.*

• *Do you see another solid that could melt if it were heated?* (students respond) *Some cheese melts when it is heated. A grilled cheese sandwich has melted cheese. Make an **X** on the cheese.*

Day 1 picture

Physical Science
- Understand that properties of solids can change when mixed, cooled, or heated

Literacy

Oral Language Development
- Name and describe pictured objects
- Respond orally to simple questions
- Use traditional structures, such as cause and effect, to convey information

Comprehension
- Recall details
- Answer questions about key details in a text read aloud

Reinforcing the Concept

Reread the Day 1 story. Then reinforce this week's science concept by discussing the story:

The students in our story told us about their lunches. What solids were in their lunches? (carrots, cheese, bread, chocolate) *What solids do you have in your lunch today?* (students respond)

Distribute the Day 2 activity. Say:

- *Look at picture 1. What do you see?* (ice cubes in a glass) *Are the ice cubes solid?* (yes) *Can they melt?* (yes) *What can make them melt?* (heat, the sun, warm air) *Find the picture that shows what happens after the ice cubes melt. Draw a line to it.*

- *Let's name the other solids in the pictures:* **ice cream**, **candle**, **butter**, **snowman**. *Look at each picture. Draw a line to show what happens after each solid melts.*

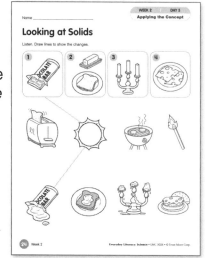

Day 2 activity

Physical Science
- Understand that properties of solids can change when mixed, cooled, or heated

Literacy

Oral Language Development
- Name and describe pictured objects
- Respond orally to simple questions
- Use traditional structures, such as cause and effect, to convey information

Applying the Concept

Distribute the Day 3 activity. Then introduce the activity by saying:

- *Look at box 1. What do you see?* (chocolate bar) *Trace the line from the chocolate to the sun. What can happen to chocolate when it gets warm?* (It can melt.) *Trace the line from the sun to the melted chocolate.*

- *Look at box 2. What do you see?* (bread and butter) *Pretend you wanted buttered toast. Toast is warm. What would you do to your bread to make it warm?* (toast it) *Draw a line to the toaster. After you put butter on the bread, what will happen to the butter?* (melt on the warm toast) *Draw a line from the toaster to the toast with melted butter.*

- *Look at box 3. What do you see?* (candles) *What can be used to light these candles?* (match) *Draw a line to the match. After a while, what would the fire do to the candles?* (melt them) *Draw a line from the match to the melted candles.*

- *Look at box 4. What do you see?* (cheese) *Mom is making cheeseburgers. She wants to grill them. What should she do?* (cook the burgers on the grill) *Draw a line to the grill. After they are cooked, the burgers are hot. What will happen if you put cheese on a hot burger?* (It will melt.) *Draw a line from the grill to the burger with melted cheese.*

Day 3 activity

Physical Science

- Understand that properties of solids can change when mixed, cooled, or heated

Literacy

Oral Language Development

- Name and describe pictured objects
- Respond orally to simple questions
- Use new vocabulary

Comprehension

- Make connections using illustrations, prior knowledge, or real-life experiences

Applying the Concept

Distribute the Day 4 activity. Then introduce the activity by saying:

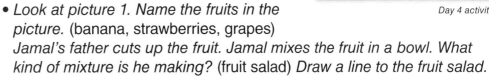

Day 4 activity

*When you mix two or more kinds of matter, you make a **mixture**. Sometimes the ingredients look different after you mix them. For example, when milk and fruit are blended to make a smoothie, the fruit is not solid and the milk is a different color. Sometimes the ingredients look the same, as when lettuce is mixed with other vegetables to make a salad. If you have ever helped in the kitchen, you have probably made a mixture!*

- *Look at picture 1. Name the fruits in the picture.* (banana, strawberries, grapes) *Jamal's father cuts up the fruit. Jamal mixes the fruit in a bowl. What kind of mixture is he making?* (fruit salad) *Draw a line to the fruit salad.*

- *Look at picture 2. What do you see?* (nuts, raisins, pretzels) *Jamal is making a snack. What kind of mixture is he making?* (trail mix) *Draw a line to the bag of trail mix.*

- *Look at picture 3. What do you see?* (lettuce, tomatoes, salad dressing) *Jamal tore up the lettuce. His dad sliced the tomatoes. What kind of mixture are they making?* (salad) *Draw a line to the salad.*

Physical Science

- Understand that properties of solids can change when mixed, cooled, or heated

Scientific Thinking & Inquiry

- Gather and record information through simple observations and investigations

Home–School Connection p. 26
Spanish version available (see p. 2)

Hands-on Science Activity

Reinforce this week's science concept with the following hands-on activity:

Materials: one plastic sandwich bag and one ice cube for each pair of students

Preparation: Assign partners. Give each pair of students an ice cube in a bag.

Activity: Introduce the activity by brainstorming ways to melt an ice cube. Then say:

We are going to have an ice cube race. When I say "Go," try to be the first team to completely melt your ice cube.

Have partners work together to melt their ice cube. Afterward, discuss some of the methods they used. (e.g., rubbing quickly, working in the sun, holding it in hands, holding it by a radiator, blowing on it, sitting on it) Then talk about which methods worked the best and why.

Looking at Solids

solid + heat = liquid

Name _____

Looking at Solids

Listen. Draw a line to show what happens when a solid melts.

1

2

3

4

5

Name _____

Looking at Solids

Listen. Draw lines to show the changes.

 1

 2

 3

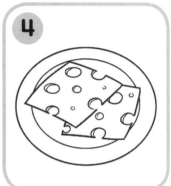 4

Everyday Literacy: Science • EMC 5026 • © Evan-Moor Corp.

Name _____

Looking at Solids

Draw a line to the correct mixture.

1

2

3

Name _____

What I Learned

Science Concept: Solids, liquids, and gases have different properties.

To Parents
This week your child learned that heat changes solids and that solids can be combined into mixtures.

What to Do
Have your child look at the picture below and name the solid each child has for his or her lunch. (carrots, cheese, bread, chocolate) Then ask your child to tell you which ones he or she has seen melt.

solid + heat = liquid

What to Do Next
Provide a supervised cooking experience for your child during which he or she can observe something melting when heat is applied to it. For example, making a quesadilla or buttering a slice of toast.

Concept

Solids, liquids, and gases have different properties.

Looking at Liquids

Science Objective:
To help students understand the liquid state of matter by observing how liquids behave

Science Vocabulary:
container, drip, flow, liquid, pour, spill, splash, spray, spread

Day 1
SKILLS

Physical Science
• Observe and describe the three states of matter
• Understand the different ways that water behaves

Literacy

Oral Language
• Respond orally to simple questions

Comprehension
• Make connections using illustrations, prior knowledge, or real-life experiences
• Answer questions about key details in a text read aloud

Introducing the Concept

Gather two clear containers of different sizes and shapes. Fill one container with water. As you pour water from the filled container into the other container, say:

• *Water is a **liquid**. I can **pour** it. A liquid flows from one place to another. A liquid has no shape of its own. It takes the shape of the container that holds it.*

• Pour a small amount of water on a flat surface and ask: *Did the water keep its shape?* (no) *No, because a liquid does not have a shape of its own.*

Listening to the Story

Distribute the Day 1 activity page to each student. Say: *Listen and look at the picture as I read a story about liquids.*

Trent was playing with his dog Quigley. They both grew thirsty, so Trent took Quigley to the kitchen. He poured water into Quigley's dish. The water took the shape of the dish, because water is a liquid. Then Trent washed his hands with liquid soap. The soap flowed into his hand from the pump. Next, while Trent was pouring lemonade into a paper cup, the cup tipped over and the lemonade spilled. The lemonade spread out and dripped onto the floor. Trent grabbed a dishcloth to wipe it up, but Quigley got to it first! He was lapping up the lemonade. It seems that Quigley's favorite liquid is lemonade!

Confirming Understanding

Reinforce the science concept by asking questions about the story. Say:

• *Look at the picture. Where do you see liquids that are in the shape of their containers?* (pitcher, soap bottle, dog dish) *Circle the containers.*

• *What spilled onto the floor?* (lemonade) *Is it still in the shape of the paper cup?* (no) *What happened?* (It spread out.) *Make an **X** on the spilled lemonade.*

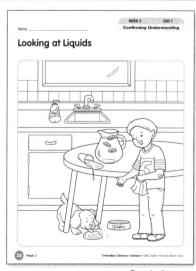

Day 1 picture

Day 2
SKILLS

Physical Science

• Observe and describe the three states of matter

• Understand the different ways that water behaves

Literacy

Oral Language Development

• Respond orally to simple questions

Comprehension

• Recall details

• Make connections using illustrations, prior knowledge, or real-life experiences

Reinforcing the Concept

Reread the Day 1 story. Then reinforce this week's science concept by guiding a discussion about the story. Say:

We learned that a liquid pours, spills, and takes the shape of its container.

Distribute the Day 2 activity. Say:

• *Point to box 1. A liquid takes the shape of its container. Does this picture show liquid in the shape of its container? Fill in the answer bubble for* **yes** *or* **no**. (yes)

• *Point to box 2. A liquid can flow. Does this picture show liquid that is flowing? Fill in the answer bubble for* **yes** *or* **no**. (yes)

• *Point to box 3. Does this picture show liquid that is flowing? Fill in the answer bubble for* **yes** *or* **no**. (no) *What shape does the liquid have?* (the shape of the soda can)

• *Point to box 4. A liquid can also spill. Does this picture show liquid that is spilling out of its container? Fill in the answer bubble for* **yes** *or* **no**. (yes)

Day 2 activity

Day 3
SKILLS

Physical Science

• Observe and describe the three states of matter

• Understand the different ways that water behaves

Literacy

Oral Language Development

• Respond orally to simple questions

• Use new vocabulary

Comprehension

• Make connections using illustrations, prior knowledge, or real-life experiences

Extending the Concept

Review the science concept by saying:

We learned that a liquid can spill and that a liquid spreads out if it is spilled. Let's talk about what else a liquid does. Have you ever jumped into a pool? (students respond) *What happened to the water?* (It splashed.)

Continue activating prior knowledge, describing how water **drips** and **sprays**. Then distribute the Day 3 activity. Say:

• *Point to number 1. The word is* **spill**. *Water can spill. Trace the word* **spill**. *Then circle the picture that shows a liquid that spilled.*

• *Point to number 2. The word is* **splash**. *Liquid can splash. Trace the word* **splash**. *Then circle the picture that shows a liquid splashing.*

• *Point to number 3. The word is* **drip**. *Liquid can drip. It can fall drop by drop. Trace the word* **drip**. *Then circle the picture that shows a liquid dripping.*

• *Point to number 4. The word is* **spray**. *Liquid can shower out in tiny drops. Trace the word* **spray**. *Then circle the picture that shows a liquid spraying.*

Day 3 activity

Physical Science
• Observe and describe the three states of matter
• Understand the different ways that water behaves

Literacy

Oral Language Development
• Respond orally to simple questions

Comprehension
• Make connections using illustrations, prior knowledge, or real-life experiences

Applying the Concept

Introduce the activity by explaining the definition of **mixture**. Say:

*You know that matter can be a solid, liquid, or gas. When two or more kinds of matter are mixed, we call this a **mixture**. Liquids can mix with other liquids or with solids.*

• *You can mix water and oats to make oatmeal. Think of some other things you have mixed. What did you make?* (students respond)

Distribute the Day 4 activity. Say:

• *Look at picture 1. What do you see?* (water, lemon juice, sugar) *What can you make if you mix these?* (lemonade) *Draw a line to the picture that shows lemonade.*

• *Look at picture 2. What do you see?* (milk, cereal) *Draw a line to the picture that shows a bowl of milk and cereal.*

• *Look at picture 3. What do you see?* (hot water, cocoa powder, marshmallows) *What can you make if you mix these?* (hot chocolate) *Draw a line to the hot chocolate.*

• *Look at picture 4. What do you see?* (liquid soap, water) *What will happen if they mix?* (They will make soapy water.) *Draw a line to the soapy water.*

Day 4 activity

Physical Science
• Observe and describe the three states of matter
• Understand the different ways that water behaves

Scientific Thinking & Inquiry
• Predict, observe, and examine different substances to determine their ability to mix with water
• Gather and record information through simple observations and investigations

Home–School Connection p. 34
Spanish version available (see p. 2)

Hands-on Science Activity

Reinforce this week's science concept with the following hands-on activity:

Materials: powdered tempera paints, water, baby food jars, paintbrushes, paper

Preparation: Place a few tablespoons of powdered paint in baby food jars, enough for two or three jars per small group of students.

Activity: Divide students into groups and provide them with the jars of different colored powders, along with paintbrushes and water. Ask:

What can you make if you mix a few drops of water with the powder? (liquid paint)

Encourage students to experiment with the powders, mixing different colors and varying amounts of water. Then say:

*We learned that a liquid can **drip**, **flow**, **pour**, **spill**, **splash**, or **spray**. Paint a picture that shows one thing a liquid can do.*

Name _____

Looking at Liquids

Everyday Literacy: Science • EMC 5026 • © Evan-Moor Corp.

Name _____

Looking at Liquids

Listen. Fill in the circle for **yes** or **no**.

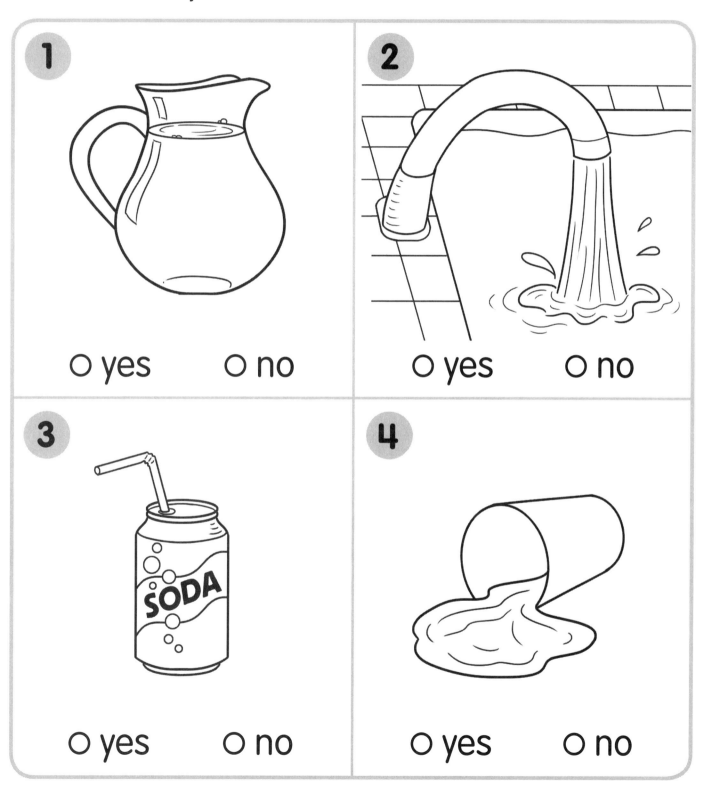

1

○ yes   ○ no

2

○ yes   ○ no

3

○ yes   ○ no

4

○ yes   ○ no

Name _____

Looking at Liquids

Listen and trace. Circle the correct picture.

1. spill

2. splash

3. drip

4. spray

Everyday Literacy: Science • EMC 5026 • © Evan-Moor Corp.

Name _____

Looking at Liquids

Listen. Draw a line to show what happens.

1  • •

2  • •

3  • •

4  • •

Name _____

What I Learned

What to Do

Ask your child to tell you what he or she knows about liquids. Then discuss what liquid does (It flows; It takes the shape of its container). Then look at the picture with your child and have him or her retell the story, pointing to and naming the liquids.

Science Concept: Solids, liquids, and gases have different properties.

To Parents

This week your child learned that liquids flow and take the shape of their container.

What to Do Next

Challenge your child to see how many liquids he or she can find in the kitchen. Write a list of the liquids with your child.

Concept

Water can change to a gas and then back to a liquid.

Where Is the Water?

Science Objective:

To help students understand that water can evaporate and it can also change back to a liquid

Science Vocabulary:

boil, evaporate, evaporation, gas, liquid, steam, water vapor

---

Day 1
SKILLS

Physical Science

• Understand that water can be a solid, a liquid, or a gas

Literacy

Oral Language Development

• Respond orally to simple questions

Comprehension

• Recall details

• Make connections using illustrations, prior knowledge, or real-life experiences

• Answer questions about key details in a text read aloud

Introducing the Concept

Activate students' prior knowledge by asking:

- *Have you ever taken a hot shower and seen steam, or tiny water droplets, rising from the water?* (students respond) *Where else have you seen steam rising?* (e.g., teakettle, hot chocolate) *Steam, or **water vapor**, is the gas form of water. Water **evaporates**, or turns from a liquid to a gas, when heated.*

- *Have you ever touched a fogged-up window? How did it feel?* (wet) *The "fog" on the glass was water vapor that had turned back to a liquid.*

Listening to the Story

Distribute the Day 1 activity page to each student. Say: *I'm going to read a story that explains how water changes to a gas and then back to a liquid.*

---

*Rosa helped her mom make chicken soup. They put chicken in a pot and filled it with water. Then they added vegetables and seasonings. Mom put the soup on the stove to cook. When the soup started boiling, a cloud of steam rose from the pot. The steam disappeared into the air. Mom said the steam was water that had **evaporated**, or changed from a liquid to a gas called **water vapor**. Now steam was forming on the kitchen window! Rosa used her finger to write her name in the steam. After she did, her finger had a drop of water on it. Mom said that when the steam hit the cool window, the vapor changed back to a liquid. That's why Rosa had a wet fingertip!*

Confirming Understanding

Reinforce the science concept by asking questions about the story. Ask:

- *What went into the air when the soup was heated?* (steam; water vapor) *Draw a circle around the steam.*

- *What happened when the steam hit the cool window?* (turned to liquid) *Make two dots on the window.*

- *What did Rosa have on her finger?* (liquid water) *Make an **X** on her finger.*

Day 1 picture

Physical Science

- Understand that water can be a solid, a liquid, or a gas

Literacy

Oral Language Development

- Respond orally to simple questions

Comprehension

- Make connections using illustrations, prior knowledge, or real-life experiences
- Answer questions about key details in a text read aloud

Reinforcing the Concept

Reread the Day 1 story. Then reinforce this week's science concept by discussing the story. Say:

- *In the story, some of the water in the pot evaporated. Where did the water go?* (into the air) *The water became a gas. When a liquid changes to a gas, it is called* **evaporation**.

- *What happened when the water vapor hit the window?* (It turned back to a liquid.)

Distribute the Day 2 activity. Ask:

- *Which picture shows what happened first?* (Mom put the pot on the stove.) *Draw a line from that picture to the number 1.*

- *Which picture shows what happened second?* (The water began to evaporate.) *Draw a line from that picture to the number 2.*

- *Which picture shows what happened third?* (The water vapor hit the window and turned to a liquid.) *Draw a line from that picture to number 3.*

- *Which picture shows what happened last?* (Rosa wrote on the window and got her finger wet.) *Draw a line from that picture to number 4.*

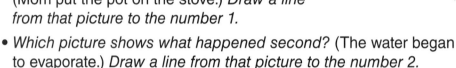

Day 2 activity

Physical Science

- Identify objects according to their physical properties
- Understand that water can be a solid, a liquid, or a gas

Literacy

Oral Language Development

- Respond orally to simple questions
- Use new vocabulary

Comprehension

- Make connections using illustrations, prior knowledge, or real-life experiences

Developing the Concept

To introduce the activity, review:

When water is heated, it evaporates. It changes from a liquid to a gas. When water vapor is cooled, it changes from a gas back to a liquid.

Distribute the Day 3 activity. Say:

- *Look at picture 1. It shows hot tea. Can you see water evaporating? Fill in the answer bubble for* **yes** *or* **no**. (yes) *How do you know water is evaporating?* (Steam is rising.)

- *Look at picture 2. What does the picture show?* (cold liquid) *Does it show water evaporating? Fill in the answer bubble for* **yes** *or* **no**. (no) *What is happening?* (Gas is turning back into a liquid.)

- *Look at box 3. Imagine that water from the hot tea is evaporating. How would you show that in this picture of hot tea?* (steam, gas) *Draw the steam.*

- *Look at box 4. Imagine that water vapor is turning back into a liquid. How would you show that on this glass of cold lemonade?* (water dripping down glass) *Draw the water dripping.*

Day 3 activity

Day 4
SKILLS

Physical Science

- Identify objects according to their physical properties
- Understand that water can be a solid, a liquid, or a gas

Literacy

Oral Language Development

- Respond orally to simple questions
- Use new vocabulary

Comprehension

- Make connections using illustrations, prior knowledge, or real-life experiences

Extending the Concept

Introduce the activity by reviewing the states of water: solid, liquid, and gas. Say:

*When water changes from a liquid to a gas, it **evaporates**. When it changes from a gas to a liquid, it **condenses**.*

*We have also learned that when water changes from a liquid to a solid, it turns to ice, or **freezes**. When water changes from a **solid** to a liquid, it **melts**.*

Distribute the Day 4 activity. Say:

- *Point to number 1. This word is **evaporate**. What does **evaporate** mean?* (It turns from a liquid to a gas.) *Draw a line from the word **evaporate** to the picture of hot water turning to vapor, or gas.*

- *Point to number 2. This word is **condense**. What happens when water condenses?* (It changes from a gas to a liquid.) *Draw a line from the word **condense** to the picture of the lemonade.*

- *Point to number 3. This word is **freeze**. What happens when water freezes?* (It becomes a solid, or ice.) *Draw a line from the word **freeze** to the picture of the frozen ice cube.*

- *Point to number 4. This word is **melt**. What happens when ice melts?* (It becomes a liquid.) *Draw a line from the word **melt** to the picture of the melting ice cube.*

Day 4 activity

Day 5
SKILLS

Physical Science

- Understand that water can be a solid, a liquid, or a gas

Scientific Thinking & Inquiry

- Gather and record information through simple observations and investigations

Home–School Connection p. 42
Spanish version available (see p. 2)

Hands-on Science Activity

Reinforce this week's science concept with the following hands-on activity:

Materials: a clear glass jar with a lid (one for each small group of students), ice cubes, paper towels

Activity: Place students in small groups. Place a few ice cubes in each group's jar. Put the lid on each jar and wipe off the outside of the jars with a paper towel. Set the jars in a warm place for a short time as students engage in another activity. Then have each group look at their jar to see what has happened. Say:

You know that the air can hold a gas called water vapor. What did we find on the outside of the jar? (water) *Where did the water come from?* (from water vapor in the air)

Have students observe the water droplets, but also encourage them to touch the outside of their jars so they can feel the water, just as Rosa from the story did.

Name _____

Where Is the Water?

Name _____

Where Is the Water?

Draw lines to show the order in which things happened.

•

•

•2

•

•3

•

•4

Name _____

Where Is the Water?

Fill in the circle for **yes** or **no**. Then draw what is missing in the bottom pictures.

1

○ yes   ○ no

2

○ yes   ○ no

3

4

Name _____

Where Is the Water?

Read each word. Listen. Draw a line to match.

1 evaporate •

•

2 condense •

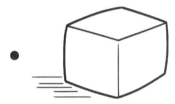

•

3 freeze •

•

4 melt •

•

Name _____

What I Learned

What to Do

Have your child look at the pictures below. Ask him or her to tell you what is happening in each one. (The heat from the stove changed the liquid water into a gas, or water vapor. The water vapor turned back into a liquid on the cool windowpane.)

Science Concept: Water evaporates and condenses.

To Parents

This week your child learned that water evaporates when heated and condenses when cooled.

What to Do Next

Have your child fill a glass with ice water and place it in a warm place. Observe what happens to the outside of the glass after it sits for a while. Have your child check the outside of the glass for condensation.

Everyday Literacy: Science • EMC 5026 • © Evan-Moor Corp.

Parts Work Together

Science Objective:
To introduce students to the idea that a system has parts that work together to do things the parts cannot do by themselves

Science Vocabulary:
part, system, together, work

Day 1
SKILLS

Physical Science
- Understand that systems have parts
- Identify parts that, when put together, can do things they cannot do by themselves

Literacy

Oral Language
- Name and describe pictured objects
- Respond orally to simple questions

Comprehension
- Make connections using illustrations, prior knowledge, or real-life experiences
- Answer questions about key details in a text read aloud

Introducing the Concept

Begin by having students look closely at their shoes. Say:

- *Look at your shoe. What parts does it have?* (e.g., heel, sole, toe, laces)
- *Why do you wear shoes?* (to keep my feet safe, help me run fast, etc.)
- *All the parts of a shoe work together to protect your feet. When all of the parts of something work together, we call it a* **system**. *The laces keep your shoe on your foot. The sole, or bottom, grips the ground. What would happen if your shoe were missing a part?* (students respond) *If one part is missing, a system won't work properly. A shoe is a system.*

Listening to the Story

Distribute the Day 1 activity page. Say: *Listen and look at the picture as I read a story about a tire swing that works as a system.*

Ted is excited about his new backyard tire swing. Ted's dad built the swing. He used a recycled tire for the seat. He put three strong chains on the tire. He hooked those three chains to another chain and attached it to a big, thick tree branch to hang the swing. All these parts are important; together, they form a **system**. *The system would not work properly without one of the parts. If the tire were missing, there would be nowhere to sit. If the chains were missing, there would be no way to hang the tire. And without the tree branch, there would be nowhere to attach the chains. Then Ted would not be able to swing! Good thing Ted's dad knows how a system for a tire swing works!*

Confirming Understanding

Reinforce the science concept by asking questions about the story. Ask:

- *What is a system?* (different parts working together to do a job) *What system did we learn about in the story?* (a tire swing)
- *What are the three main parts of the tire swing system?* (tree branch, chains, tire) *Make an* **X** *on the part that you sit on.*
- *What would happen if the chains were missing?* (There would be no way to hang the swing.) *Color the chains.*

Day 1 picture

Physical Science

- Understand that systems have parts

- Identify parts that, when put together, can do things they cannot do by themselves

Literacy

Oral Language Development

- Name and describe pictured objects

- Respond orally to simple questions

Comprehension

- Make connections using illustrations, prior knowledge, or real-life experiences

- Answer questions about key details in a text read aloud

Reinforcing the Concept

Reread the Day 1 story. Then reinforce this week's science concept by guiding a discussion about the story. Say:

We learned that a system is made of parts that work together. What system did Ted's dad build in the backyard? (tire swing)

Distribute the Day 2 activity. Say:

- *The words next to the swing name the parts of the tire swing system. Point to each word as you read along with me: **tire, chains, tree**.*

- *Look at the picture. Which part of the system do the chains hang from?* (tree) *Draw a line from the picture of the tree to the word **tree**.*

- *Which part of the swing connects the tire to the tree?* (chains) *Draw a line from the picture of the chains to the word **chains**.*

- *Which part of the swing will Ted sit on?* (tire) *Draw a line from the picture of the tire to the word **tire**.*

- *The sentence reads: **A swing is a system.** Trace the two words.*

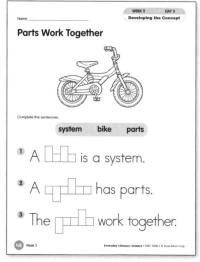

Day 2 activity

Physical Science

- Understand that systems have parts

- Identify parts that, when put together, can do things they cannot do by themselves

Literacy

Oral Language Development

- Name and describe pictured objects

- Respond orally to simple questions

Comprehension

- Make connections using illustrations, prior knowledge, or real-life experiences

Developing the Concept

To introduce the activity, review the definition of a system. Say:

The parts of a system work together to do something. Can you name a system that you or someone in your family use at home? (e.g., video game, stereo, oven)

Distribute the Day 3 activity. Say:

What does this picture show? (a bike) *A bike is another kind of system. When we ride it, it moves us from place to place. Can you name the parts of the bike?* (wheels, seat, pedals, chains, handlebars, brakes)

- *Now point to each word in the gray box as I read it: **system, bike, parts**. Let's use the words to complete the sentences about the bike.*

- *Sentence 1 says: **A _____ is a system.** Which word completes the sentence?* (bike) *Write **bike** in the boxes.*

- *Sentence 2 says: **A _____ has parts.** Which word completes the sentence?* (system) *Write **system** in the boxes.*

- *Sentence 3 says: **The _____ work together.** Which word completes the sentence?* (parts) *Write **parts** in the boxes.*

Day 3 activity

Day 4
SKILLS

Physical Science
- Understand that systems have parts
- Identify parts that, when put together, can do things they cannot do by themselves

Literacy

Oral Language Development
- Respond orally to simple questions

Comprehension
- Recall details
- Make connections using illustrations, prior knowledge, or real-life experiences

Applying the Concept

Introduce the activity by saying:

Name two systems you have learned about this week. (swing, bike) *Name the parts of each system.* (tire, chains, tree; wheels, seat, pedals, chains, handlebars, brakes)

Distribute the Day 4 activity. Say:

Listen to these clues about other systems.

- *Point to sentence 1. Move your finger under each word as we read together: **I can pull it.** Which picture shows a system that you can pull?* (wagon) *Name the parts you see.* (wheels, handle, body) *Draw a line to the picture of the wagon.*

- *Read sentence 2: **It heats a home.** Which system heats a home?* (fireplace) *What are its parts?* (bricks, logs, chimney) *Draw a line to the picture of the fireplace.*

- *Read sentence 3: **It tells time.** Which system tells time?* (clock) *What are its parts?* (hands, face, numbers) *Draw a line to the picture of the clock.*

- *Read sentence 4: **It holds up my body.** Which system holds up your body?* (skeleton) *What are its parts?* (bones) *Draw a line to the picture of the skeleton.*

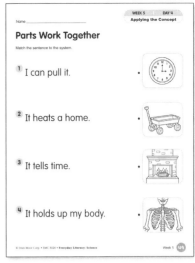

Day 4 activity

Day 5
SKILLS

Physical Science
- Understand that systems have parts

Scientific Thinking & Inquiry
- Design a simple system
- Manipulate a system so that when a part is separated from the whole, the system fails

---

Home–School Connection p. 50
Spanish version available (see p. 2)

Hands-on Science Activity

Reinforce this week's science concept with the following hands-on activity:

Materials: building blocks or bricks, hardcover books, toy cars

Preparation: Have students work in pairs. Provide each pair with two blocks or bricks, a book, and a toy car.

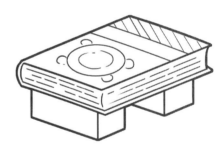

Activity: Introduce the activity by discussing the notion of a bridge as a system. Ask:

*Have you ever been on a bridge? A bridge is a **system**. There are many types of bridges, but the simplest bridge has two basic parts: the part you walk or drive on called the deck, and the part that holds up the deck called the footing or post. Let's build a simple bridge.*

Model placing a book across two blocks or bricks and have students do the same. Invite them to drive their cars across the deck. Ask:

What does each part of your bridge do? (book is the "deck"; blocks are the "supports") *What would happen if one of the parts were missing?* (If a support were missing, the bridge would collapse. If the deck were missing, the car wouldn't be able to get across.)

Name _____

Parts Work Together

Name _____

Parts Work Together

Draw a line to each part of the tire swing. Then read the sentence and trace the words.

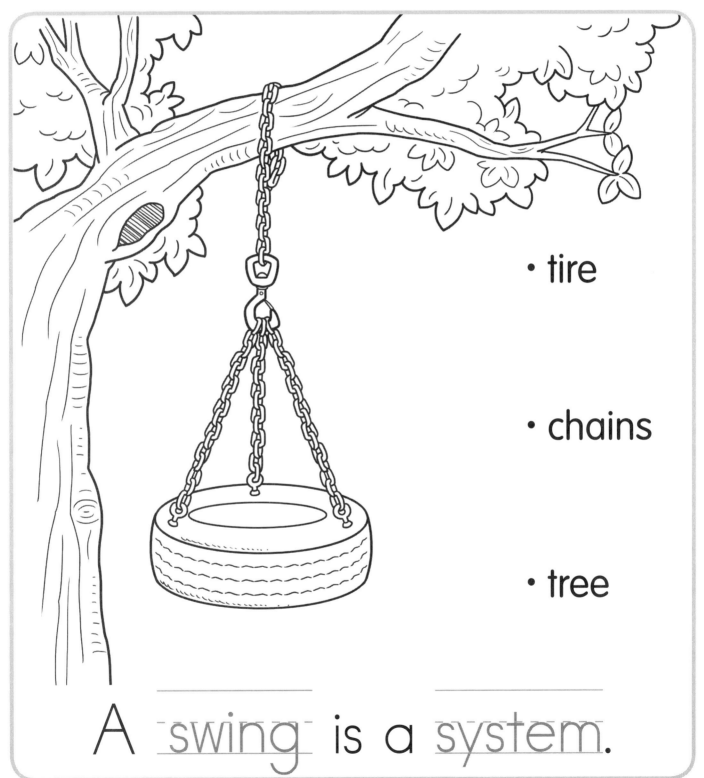

- tire

- chains

- tree

A ̲s̲w̲i̲n̲g̲ is a ̲s̲y̲s̲t̲e̲m̲.

Name _____

Parts Work Together

Complete the sentences.

system	bike	parts

1 A ⬜⬜ is a system.

2 A ⬜⬜ has parts.

3 The ⬜⬜ work together.

Everyday Literacy: Science • EMC 5026 • © Evan-Moor Corp.

Name _____

Parts Work Together

Match the sentence to the system.

1 I can pull it.

2 It heats a home.

3 It tells time.

4 It holds up my body.

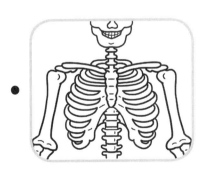

Name _____

What I Learned

What to Do
Have your child look at the picture of the tire swing system below and have him or her name the parts of a tire swing. Have your child trace each word. Then discuss what would happen if a part were missing.

WEEK 5

Home–School Connection

Science Concept: A system has parts that work together.

To Parents
This week your child learned that a swing is a system with parts that work together.

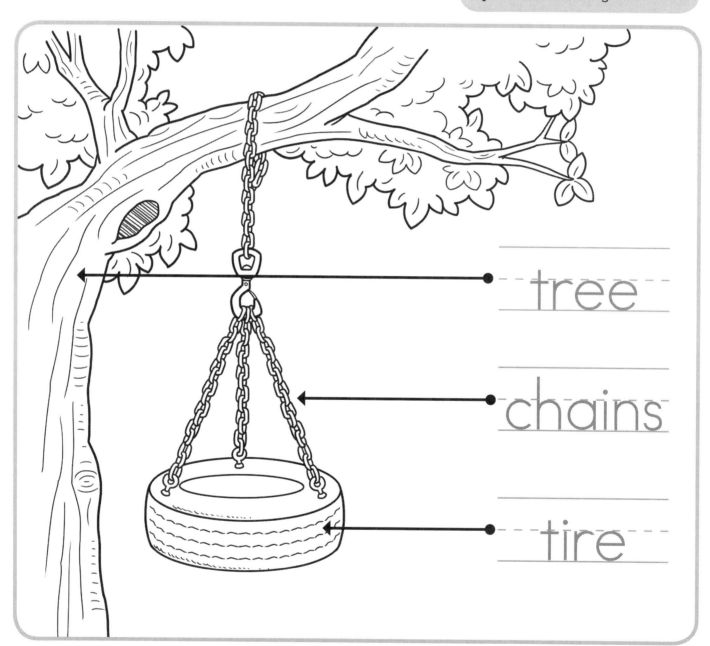

tree

chains

tire

What to Do Next
Help your child find objects around the house that are simple systems and name their parts. For example, a fireplace, a lamp, a camera, a book, a bicycle, a clock, a skateboard, and so on.

Concept

Sound is made by vibrating objects.

Making Sound

Science Objective:
To help students understand that sound is made by vibrating objects, and that sound travels through the air

Science Vocabulary:
move, sound, sound wave, travel, vibrate, vibrations

Day 1 SKILLS

Investigation

- Identify objects that create specific sounds
- Understand how sound is made

Literacy

Oral Language Development

- Respond orally to simple questions

Comprehension

- Make connections using illustrations, prior knowledge, or real-life experiences
- Answer questions about key details in a text read aloud
- Make inferences and draw conclusions

Introducing the Concept

Gather a rubber band, a ruler, and a pencil. Stretch the rubber band across the ruler; push the pencil under the rubber band. Have students listen and observe the movement of the rubber band as you pluck it. Ask:

- *What do you hear when I pluck the rubber band?* (a twang or a buzzing sound)
- *What do you see?* (the rubber band moving)
- *The rubber band shakes quickly back and forth. We say it **vibrates**. Vibration causes sound. Can you name some musical instruments with strings that vibrate?* (guitar, violin, harp, etc.)

Listening to the Story

Distribute the Day 1 activity page. Say: *Listen and look at the picture as I read a story about a girl who experiments with sound.*

Sumiko wanted to learn more about sound. She made a drum out of a coffee can and a balloon. She cut the balloon and stretched it over the top of the empty can. Then she put a rubber band around the can to hold the balloon. Next, she poured some sugar onto the center of the balloon. She got a metal pan and banged on it with a spoon. "What's going on?" asked her dad when he heard the noise. Sumiko said, "Look! I can make the sugar dance without touching it!" How did she do that? **Sound waves** *from the metal pan traveled through the air. They made the balloon vibrate, and that made the sugar move. Sumiko could see sound waves in action!*

Confirming Understanding

Reinforce the science concept by asking questions about the story. Ask:

- *How did Sumiko make noise?* (by banging on a metal pan with a spoon) *Circle the pan.*
- *How did the sound waves travel?* (through the air) *Did the sound waves make the balloon vibrate?* (yes)
- *What made the sugar move?* (the vibrating balloon) *Draw an arrow to where the sugar is dancing!*

Day 1 picture

Investigation
• Understand how sound is made

Literacy

Oral Language Development
• Respond orally to simple questions
• Use new vocabulary

Comprehension
• Answer questions about key details in a text read aloud

Reinforcing the Concept

Reread the Day 1 story. Then reinforce this week's science concept by discussing the story. Say:

In the story, Sumiko did not actually see the sound waves, but she knew they were there. How did she know? (The sound waves made the balloon vibrate, which made the sugar dance.)

Distribute the Day 2 activity. Say:

- *Look at the pictures in the box. In the story, which things vibrated? (pan, drum) Circle those pictures.*

- *Now look at sentence 1. It says, **The pan vibrates**, or shakes quickly back and forth. Now let's read it together: **The pan vibrates**. Trace the word **vibrates**.*

- *Sentence 2 says, **The pan makes a sound.** Now let's read it together: **The pan makes a sound.** Trace the word **sound**.*

- *Sentence 3 says, **Sound waves travel.** Now let's read it together: **Sound waves travel.** Trace the word **travel**.*

Day 2 activity

Investigation
• Identify objects that create specific sounds
• Understand how sound is made

Literacy

Oral Language Development
• Respond orally to simple questions
• Use new vocabulary

Comprehension
• Make connections using illustrations, prior knowledge, or real-life experiences

Applying the Concept

Introduce the activity by displaying photos or illustrations of musical instruments. Say:

Sound waves are vibrations that travel through the air. We can make musical instruments vibrate to make different sounds.

- *What instruments make a sound by being hit? (e.g., triangle, drum, bell)*

- *What instruments can you think of that make a sound by being plucked? (e.g., harp, guitar, banjo, bass, ukulele)*

Distribute the Day 3 activity. Say:

There are many ways to make a musical instrument vibrate to make a sound.

- *Point to number 1. Let's read the word together: **hit**. Which musical instrument vibrates when you **hit** it? (drum) Draw a line to the drum.*

- *Let's read the next word: **pluck**. Which musical instrument vibrates when you **pluck** the strings? (guitar) Draw a line to the guitar.*

- *Let's read word 3: **blow**. Which musical instrument vibrates when you **blow** into it? (horn, trumpet) Draw a line to the trumpet.*

- *Let's read word 4: **shake**. Which musical instrument vibrates when you **shake** it? (maracas, shakers) Draw a line to the maracas.*

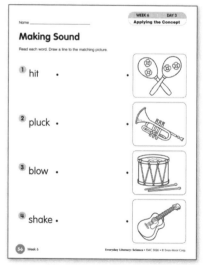

Day 3 activity

Day 4 SKILLS

Investigation
• Identify objects that create specific sounds

Literacy

Oral Language Development
• Use new vocabulary

Comprehension
• Recall details
• Make connections using illustrations, prior knowledge, or real-life experiences

Applying the Concept

Review this week's science concept by saying:
We have been learning about sound.

- *What is a fast back-and-forth movement called?* (vibration)
- *How is sound made?* (by objects vibrating)
- *What happens if you pluck the string on a guitar?* (string vibrates; makes sound)

Then distribute the Day 4 activity. Say:

- *Point to number 1. This word is **ding**. Trace the letters. Which musical instrument makes this sound?* (bell) *Draw a line from the word **ding** to the bell.*
- *Point to number 2. This word is **toot**. Trace the letters. Which instrument makes this sound?* (horn) *Draw a line from the word **toot** to the horn.*
- *Point to number 3. This word is **twang**. Trace the letters. Which instrument makes this sound?* (guitar) *Draw a line from the word **twang** to the guitar.*
- *Point to number 4. This word is **boom**. Trace the letters. Which instrument makes this sound?* (bass drum) *Draw a line from the word **boom** to the drum.*

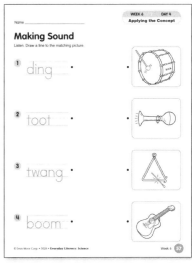

Day 4 activity

Day 5 SKILLS

Investigation
• Understand how sound is made

Literacy

Oral Language Development
• Respond orally to simple questions

Scientific Thinking & Inquiry
• Gather and record information through simple observations and investigations

Home–School Connection p. 58
Spanish version available (see p. 2)

Hands-on Science Activity

Reinforce this week's science concept with the following hands-on activity:

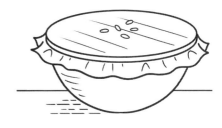

Materials: mixing bowl, plastic wrap, rubber band, uncooked rice, and an assortment of noisemakers, such as cookie tins, spoons, whistles, etc.

Preparation: Stretch the plastic wrap over the mixing bowl and secure with a rubber band. Place a few grains of rice on the surface of the drum.

Activity: Introduce the activity by asking:

Do you remember Sumiko's experiment with the drum? Let's try that experiment ourselves. Let's make rice dance!

Invite volunteers to get close to the drum. Have them make different noises, such as clanging a pot, clapping, blowing a whistle, or singing. Prompt students to observe and record the effect of the different noises on the rice:

- *Did the loudness of the sound make the rice dance more or less?*
- *Did it matter how close you were to the drum or how far away you were from the drum?*
- *What other sounds would be fun to try? How do you predict that they would make the rice dance?*

Name _____

Making Sound

Name _____

Making Sound

Circle the things that vibrate in the story.

Read the sentences. Trace the words.

1 The pan vibrates.

2 The pan makes a sound.

3 Sound waves travel.

Making Sound

Read each word. Draw a line to the matching picture.

1 hit •

2 pluck •

3 blow •

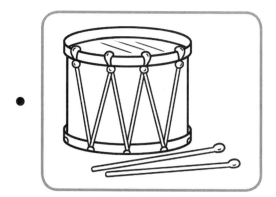

4 shake •

Name _____

Making Sound

Listen. Draw a line to the matching picture.

1  •

•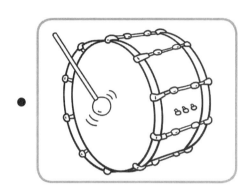

2  •

•

3  •

•

4  •

•

Name _____

What I Learned

What to Do

Have your child look at the picture below. Ask him or her to describe what is happening. (The girl is demonstrating that a bit of sugar on top of a homemade drum moves when she makes a noise with the pan. It shows that sound waves are vibrations.) Then have your child color the picture.

Science Concept: Sound is made by vibrating objects.

To Parents
This week your child learned how sound is made.

What to Do Next

Help your child make a simple guitar by stretching a rubber band lengthwise around a wooden ruler. Push a pencil under the rubber band. Ask your child to experiment with moving the pencil to see how the sound changes.

Everyday Literacy: Science • EMC 5026 • © Evan-Moor Corp.

Where Animals Live

Science Objective:
To help students understand that habitats provide animals with the things they need to survive

Science Vocabulary:
cactus, den, desert, forest, habitat, nest, ocean, protects, shelter, survive

Day 1
SKILLS

Life Science

• Understand that people, plants, and animals are living things with basic needs

• Understand that animals inhabit many different places

• Identify ways in which an animal's habitat provides for its basic needs

Literacy
Oral Language Development

• Respond orally to simple questions

• Use new vocabulary

Comprehension

• Make connections using illustrations, prior knowledge, or real-life experiences

• Answer questions about key details in a text read aloud

Introducing the Concept

Explain that a place where an animal lives, eats, and sleeps is called its **habitat**. Then explain that different animals survive, or stay alive, in different habitats. Say:

• *A **forest** is one kind of habitat. It has many trees. Animals such as bears and deer live in forests. Have you ever been in a forest? What animals or plants did you see?* (students respond)

• *Another kind of habitat is a **desert**. It is very dry there. It is usually hot during the day and cold at night. What animals or plants can you think of that might live in the desert?* (snakes, lizards, cactuses, etc.)

Listening to the Story

Direct students' attention to the Day 1 activity page. Say: *Listen and look at the picture as I read a story about an animal that lives in a desert.*

I have a new book about desert animals. My favorite story is about a bird called the elf owl. It lives in a hole in a cactus. The hole was made by another bird—a woodpecker. The hole is high up in the prickly cactus. This keeps the elf owl safe from other animals. It also protects the owl from the hot sun. When the elf owl gets hungry, it leaves the cactus and searches for food. It eats insects near desert flowers. Then it comes back to its shelter in the hole in the cactus. Not every animal can survive in the desert, but the elf owl is right at home!

Confirming Understanding

Reinforce the science concept by asking students questions about the story. Ask:

• *Who lives in a hole in the cactus?* (elf owl) *Circle the elf owl. Why is the hole a good shelter?* (high up; keeps the owl safe and cool)

• *Which animal made the hole?* (woodpecker) *Circle the woodpecker.*

• *Where might the elf owl find food?* (near a flower) *Find the insect that is near the flower. Circle it. Then write the word **desert** in the boxes.*

Day 1 picture

Day 2
SKILLS

Life Science

• Understand that people, plants, and animals are living things with basic needs

• Understand that animals inhabit many different places

• Identify ways in which an animal's habitat provides for its basic needs

Literacy

Oral Language Development

• Respond orally to simple questions

• Use new vocabulary

Comprehension

• Answer questions about key details in a text read aloud

• Make inferences and draw conclusions

Reinforcing the Concept

Reread the Day 1 story. Then reinforce this week's science concept by comparing shelter in a desert habitat to shelter in a forest habitat. Explain:

An elf owl lives in a cactus for shelter. The trees in a forest habitat provide shelter for forest animals.

Then distribute the Day 2 activity and say:

• *Look at the picture. Some animals use trees for shelter. What animal do you see peeking out from a hole high in the tree? (squirrel) Circle the squirrel.*

• *Some animals make **nests** in forest trees. What animal do you see on a nest? (bird) Circle the bird.*

• *Some animals live in **dens**, or hiding places on the ground. Dens are often in piles of rocks or at the bottom of a tree. What animal do you see in its den? (fox) Make an **X** on the fox.*

• *Now point to the sentence under the picture. Move your finger under the words and read along with me: **A forest is a habitat.** Trace the word **forest** with your finger. Now write the word **forest** in the boxes.*

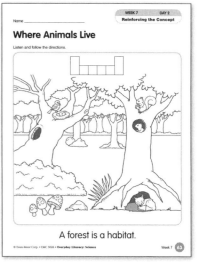

Day 2 activity

Day 3
SKILLS

Life Science

• Understand that people, plants, and animals are living things with basic needs

• Understand that animals inhabit many different places

• Identify ways in which an animal's habitat provides for its basic needs

Literacy

Oral Language Development

• Respond orally to simple questions

• Use new vocabulary

Comprehension

• Make connections using illustrations, prior knowledge, or real-life experiences

Applying the Concept

Distribute the Day 3 activity and markers. Review the features of desert and forest habitats. Then introduce an ocean habitat. Ask:

What do you know about the ocean? (students respond) Many animals find food and shelter in the ocean. Some animals swim near the top. Some animals swim along the bottom. Some animals hide behind rocks or between plants. Let's find some ocean animals in this picture.

• *A **shark** is a big fish. It has sharp teeth for eating other fish. Where is the shark in this picture? (swimming near the top of the picture) Circle the shark.*

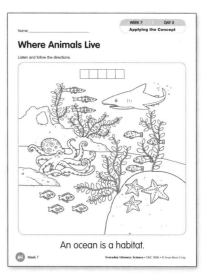

Day 3 activity

• *A **sea star** is sometimes called a **starfish** because it is star-shaped. But it is <u>not</u> a fish! It clings to rocks and moves very slowly. Find one sea star and color it orange.*

• *An **octopus** lives at the bottom of the ocean. It has eight arms that help it move. Find the octopus. Make a dot on each arm as we count out loud.*

• ***Kelp** is a tall, wavy plant that grows up from the bottom of the ocean. Many animals eat kelp. Color a piece of kelp green.*

• *Now point to the sentence under the picture. Move your finger under the words and read along with me: **An ocean is a habitat.** Trace the word **ocean** with your finger. Now write the word **ocean** in the boxes.*

Life Science

- Understand that people, plants, and animals are living things with basic needs
- Understand that animals inhabit many different places
- Identify ways in which an animal's habitat provides for its basic needs

Literacy

Oral Language Development

- Respond orally to simple questions
- Use new vocabulary

Comprehension

- Recall details
- Make connections using illustrations, prior knowledge, or real-life experiences

Applying the Concept

Distribute the Day 4 activity and review:

We have learned about three habitats: the desert, the forest, and the ocean.

- *What are some things that live or grow in the desert?* (owl, cactus, etc.)
- *What are some things that live or grow in the forest?* (fox, tree, etc.)
- *What are some things that live or grow in the ocean?* (shark, kelp, etc.)

Guide students through the activity:

- *Look at the word box at the top of the page. Move your finger under the words and read along with me:* **desert, forest, ocean.**
- *Now look at the pictures. Point to the picture that shows a desert. Name some things you see in the picture.* (cactus, owl, sun) *Write the word* **desert** *in the boxes.*
- *Find the picture of the forest. Name some things you see in the picture.* (nest, hole, den) *Write the word* **forest** *in the boxes.*
- *Find the picture of the ocean. What animals do you see?* (shark, octopus, sea star) *Write the word* **ocean** *in the boxes.*
- *Now draw an animal that lives in each habitat. Then color each habitat.*

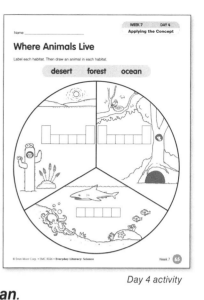

Day 4 activity

Life Science

- Understand that people, plants, and animals are living things with basic needs
- Understand that animals inhabit many different places

Home–School Connection p. 66
Spanish version available (see p. 2)

Hands-on Science Activity

Reinforce this week's science concept with the following hands-on activity:

Materials: green modeling clay (or air-dry polymer clay), red beads, picture of saguaro cactus, forks, shallow container of sand or rice

Activity: Give each student a ball of clay and red beads. Guide the activity by showing a picture of the saguaro cactus and saying:

- *This is a picture of a saguaro cactus. A saguaro cactus provides food and shelter for many desert animals, including the elf owl. You are going to make a mini cactus.*
- *Look at the picture and then shape the clay into a cactus.*
- *The cactus has red fruit. Bats and other animals eat this cactus fruit. Add beads to your cactus for the fruit. Then poke a hole in your cactus for an elf owl to live in.*
- *A saguaro cactus has grooves. Use a fork to make the grooves in your cactus.*

When students are satisfied with their cactuses, have them arrange them in a shallow container of sand or other suitable material.

Name _____

Where Animals Live

Name _____

Where Animals Live

Listen and follow the directions.

A forest is a habitat.

Name _____

Where Animals Live

Listen and follow the directions.

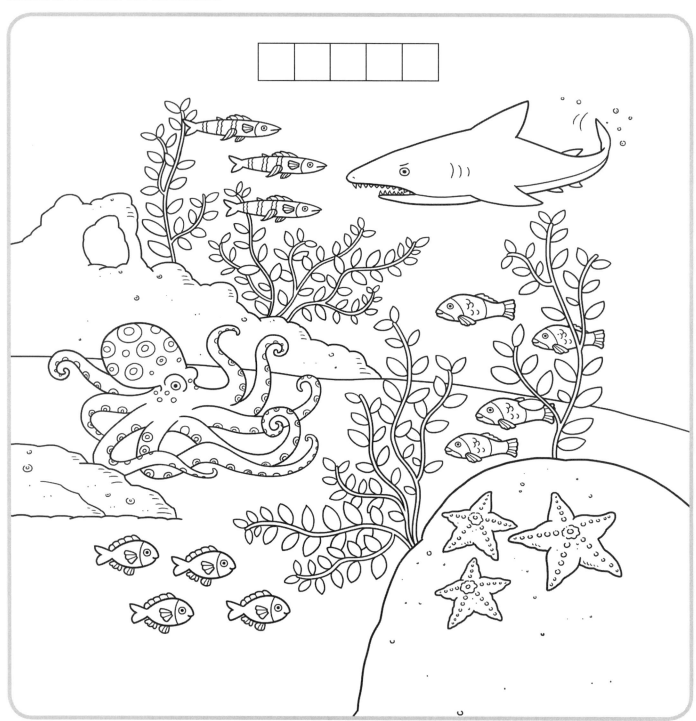

An ocean is a habitat.

Name _____

Where Animals Live

Label each habitat. Then draw an animal in each habitat.

desert   forest   ocean

Name _____

What I Learned

What to Do
Have your child look at the picture below. Ask him or her to tell you details about the desert habitat shown. Then have him or her color the picture.

WEEK 7

Home–School Connection

Science Concept: Animals inhabit different kinds of environments.

To Parents
This week your child learned about desert, forest, and ocean habitats.

What to Do Next
Take a discovery walk with your child. Help your child make a list of animals you see. Look for animals' homes along your walk.

Plants Are Food

Science Objective:
To help students understand that plants are an important food source

Science Vocabulary:
flower, fruit, leaves, plant, root, seed, stem, vegetable

Day 1
SKILLS

Life Science
• Identify and describe the parts of a plant

Literacy

Oral Language Development
• Respond orally to simple questions

Comprehension
• Recall details
• Make connections using illustrations, prior knowledge, or real-life experiences
• Answer questions about key details in a text read aloud

Introducing the Concept

Bring in a plant or a picture of a plant and display it as you review the parts of a plant (roots, stem, leaf, flower, fruit, seed). Then say:

Vegetables, fruits, and seeds are parts of plants. Name some vegetables, fruits, or seeds that you like to eat. (students respond)

Listening to the Story

Distribute the Day 1 activity page to each student. Say: *Listen and look at the picture as I read a story about children who learn about plant parts they eat.*

Jasmine's class is learning that fruits and vegetables are the roots, stems, leaves, flowers, and fruits of different plants. The teacher asked the students to bring fruits and vegetables in their lunches. Jasmine brought carrots. The carrot is the root of a carrot plant. Maya brought asparagus. Asparagus is the stem of an asparagus plant. Nicole brought lettuce. She already knew that lettuce is the leaf of a lettuce plant. Emilio brought an apple, which is the fruit of an apple tree. Alex brought broccoli and told the teacher, "This doesn't look like a flower, but it is! It is the flower of a broccoli plant!" Brian brought a pack of crunchy sunflower seeds. "I know these aren't fruits or vegetables," he said. "But seeds are also part of a plant."

Confirming Understanding

Reinforce the science concept by asking questions about the story. Ask:

Day 1 picture

• *What does Jasmine have for lunch?* (carrots) *What part of the plant are they?* (roots) *Color them orange.*

• *Maya has asparagus for lunch. What part of the plant is it?* (stem) *Color it green.*

• *Which vegetable is a leaf?* (lettuce) *Circle it. Which food is a fruit?* (apple) *Draw a line under it. Which food is a flower bud?* (broccoli) *Make an X on it.*

• *What part of a plant are sunflower seeds?* (seeds) *Color the seeds brown.*

Life Science

• Identify and describe the parts of a plant

Literacy

Oral Language Development

• Respond orally to simple questions

• Use new vocabulary

Comprehension

• Recall details

• Make connections using illustrations, prior knowledge, or real-life experiences

• Answer questions about key details in a text read aloud

Reinforcing the Concept

Reread the Day 1 story. Then reinforce this week's science concept by guiding a discussion about the story. Say:

Our story was about plant parts we eat. What did the children in the story bring for lunch that came from plants? (carrots, asparagus, lettuce, apple, sunflower seeds, broccoli)

Distribute the Day 2 activity. Say:

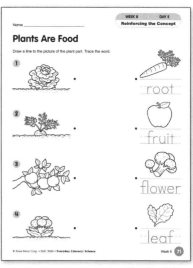

Day 2 activity

• *Point to number 1. This picture shows a lettuce plant. Which part of a lettuce plant can you eat?* (leaf) *Draw a line to the picture of the lettuce leaf. Trace the word* **leaf**.

• *Point to number 2. This picture shows a carrot plant. Which part of a carrot plant can you eat?* (root) *Draw a line to the picture of the carrot. Trace the word* **root**.

• *Point to number 3. This picture shows an apple tree branch. Which part of an apple tree can you eat?* (fruit) *Draw a line to the picture of the apple. Trace the word* **fruit**.

Repeat the process with the broccoli plant.

Life Science

• Identify and describe the parts of a plant

Literacy

Oral Language Development

• Respond orally to simple questions

Comprehension

• Make connections using illustrations, prior knowledge, or real-life experiences

Applying the Concept

Distribute the Day 3 activity. Then introduce the activity by saying:

These pictures tell the story of corn, from the time it grows in the field to the time it gets to your table. Have you ever seen corn growing in a field? Have you seen ears of corn neatly piled at the grocery store? When you bring the corn home, what part do you eat? Do you like corn on the cob or just the corn kernels? Think of how corn gets to your table as we put the pictures in order.

Day 3 activity

• *What happens first? How does corn get its start?* (seeds get planted) *Find that picture and write* **1** *in the box.*

• *Which picture shows what happens next?* (the seeds growing into corn plants) *Find that picture and write* **2** *in the box.*

• *Which picture shows what happens next?* (corn being picked) *Find that picture and write* **3** *in the box.*

• *Finally, you eat the seeds! Write* **4** *in that box.*

Day 4
SKILLS

Life Science

• Identify and describe the parts of a plant

Literacy

Oral Language Development

• Respond orally to simple questions

Comprehension

• Make inferences and draw conclusions

Extending the Concept

Distribute the Day 4 activity. Introduce the activity by having students name their favorite fruits. Then say:

Fruit is the part of the plant that contains the plant's **seeds***. Some foods that we call vegetables are actually fruits!*

Day 4 activity

   • *Look at picture 1. What food is this? (a tomato) Does a tomato have seeds? (yes) Is a tomato a fruit? Fill in the answer bubble for* **yes** *or* **no***.* (yes)

   • *Look at picture 2. What food is this? (a lemon) Does a lemon have seeds? (yes) Is a lemon a fruit? Fill in the answer bubble for* **yes** *or* **no***.* (yes)

   • *Look at picture 3. What food is this?* (a potato) *Does a potato have seeds?* (no) *Is a potato a fruit? Fill in the answer bubble for* **yes** *or* **no***.* (no)

   • *Look at picture 4. Does a watermelon have seeds?* (yes) *Is a watermelon a fruit? Fill in the answer bubble for* **yes** *or* **no***.* (yes)

   • *Look at picture 5. Does a cucumber have seeds?* (yes) *Is a cucumber a fruit? Fill in the answer bubble for* **yes** *or* **no***.* (yes)

   • *Look at picture 6. This is spinach. Does spinach have seeds?* (no) *Is spinach a fruit? Fill in the answer bubble for* **yes** *or* **no***.* (no)

Day 5
SKILLS

Life Science

• Identify and describe the parts of a plant

Scientific Thinking & Inquiry

• Sort objects according to common characteristics

• Gather and record information through simple observations and investigations

• Interpret information found in charts

Home–School Connection p. 74
Spanish version available (see p. 2)

Hands-on Science Activity

Reinforce this week's science concept with the following hands-on activity:

Materials: pictures of edible plants clipped from garden catalogs or from free online clip art sources (USDA.gov, for example), chart paper

Activity: Draw a chart with six rows on the paper. Label the rows **root, stem, leaf, flower, fruit, seed**. Place the chart where students can easily reach it. Distribute one picture to partners and have them discuss it. Then say:

You know that people eat different parts of plants. Look at your picture. Can you or your partner name the plant? Which part or parts of the plant can be eaten?

Have partners tell the class the name of their plant and what part can be eaten. For example, *This is lettuce; We eat the leaves.* If the class agrees with the classification, have students tape the picture in the correct row on the chart.

Name _____

Plants Are Food

We get food from plants.

     Everyday Literacy: Science • EMC 5026 • © Evan-Moor Corp.

Name _____

Plants Are Food

Draw a line to the picture of the plant part. Trace the word.

1

root

2

fruit

3

flower

4

leaf

Name _____

Plants Are Food

Number the pictures to show the correct order.

Everyday Literacy: Science • EMC 5026 • © Evan-Moor Corp.

Name _____

Plants Are Food

Listen. Fill in the circle for **yes** or **no**.

1 ○ yes   ○ no

2 ○ yes   ○ no

3 ○ yes   ○ no

4 ○ yes   ○ no

5 ○ yes   ○ no

6 ○ yes   ○ no

Name _____

What I Learned

What to Do
Have your child look at the picture below. Talk about the fruits, vegetables, and seeds the children are holding. (carrots, asparagus, lettuce, broccoli, apple, sunflower seeds) Have your child tell you what part of a plant each food is. (root, stem, leaf, flower, fruit, seed)

Science Concept: People eat different parts of plants.

To Parents
This week your child learned about the different parts of plants that people eat.

We get food from plants.

What to Do Next
Help your child find foods at home that are parts of plants. Ask him or her to sort them into categories according to which part of the plant they are.

What Do Animals Eat?

Science Objective:

To help students understand that some animals are carnivores (meat eaters), some are herbivores (plant eaters), and some are omnivores (meat and plant eaters)

Science Vocabulary:

bite, carnivore, chew, graze, grind, herbivore, omnivore, tear, teeth

Day 1
SKILLS

Life Science

• Understand that people, plants, and animals are living things with basic needs

• Infer what animals eat from the shapes of their teeth

Literacy

Oral Language Development

• Respond orally to simple questions

Comprehension

• Recall details

• Make connections using illustrations, prior knowledge, or real-life experiences

• Answer questions about key details in a text read aloud

• Make inferences and draw conclusions

Introducing the Concept

Activate prior knowledge by inviting students who have pets or take care of farm animals to describe what foods the animals like to eat. Then say:

• *Some animals eat meat. A meat eater is called a* **carnivore**. *Some animals eat plants. An animal that eats plants is called an* **herbivore**. *Other animals eat both meat and plants. They are called* **omnivores**.

• *Are you a carnivore, an herbivore, or an omnivore?* (students respond)

Listening to the Story

Distribute the Day 1 activity page. Say: *Listen and look at the picture as I read a story about a boy's two pets.*

I have two very different pets. Pepper is a **carnivore***, or a meat eater. His teeth are sharp and pointed. He uses them to bite and tear meat. Pepper gets excited when I give him a bone or a piece of ham. Can you guess what Pepper is? He is my dog! My other pet is Pickles. She is an* **herbivore***. She eats only plants. Her teeth are flat and wide for chewing and grinding hay. She also likes to graze on grass. Pickles shows her teeth when I feed her. Pickles is my pony! Pickles and Pepper have different kinds of teeth, but I have both kinds. That's because I'm an* **omnivore***: I eat everything!*

Confirming Understanding

Reinforce the science concept by asking students questions about the story. Ask:

• *Is Pepper a carnivore or an herbivore?* (carnivore) *Why are Pepper's teeth sharp and pointed?* (to bite and tear meat) *Make a black dot on Pepper's bone.*

• *Is Pickles a carnivore or an herbivore?* (herbivore) *Why are Pickles' teeth flat and wide?* (to chew and grind hay) *Make a green* **X** *on the hay.*

• *Is the boy a carnivore, an herbivore, or an omnivore?* (omnivore) *Circle the boy's mouth.*

Day 1 picture

Life Science

- Understand that people, plants, and animals are living things with basic needs
- Infer what animals eat from the shapes of their teeth

Literacy

Oral Language Development

- Respond orally to simple questions

Comprehension

- Recall details
- Answer questions about key details in a text read aloud

Reinforcing the Concept

Reread the Day 1 story. Then reinforce this week's science concept by discussing the story:

Our story was about the kinds of foods that animals eat.

- *What does the dog like to eat?* (meat, bone, ham)
- *What does the pony like to eat?* (hay, grass)

Distribute the Day 2 activity. Say:

- *Point to box 1. Meat-eating animals have sharp teeth. Does a dog have sharp teeth? Fill in the answer bubble for **yes** or **no**.* (yes) *What are sharp teeth for?* (for biting and tearing)

- *Point to box 2. Do a dog and a pony eat the same food? Fill in the answer bubble for **yes** or **no**.* (no)

- *Point to box 3. What does this pony eat?* (plants, hay, grass) *Is this pony an **herbivore**? Fill in the answer bubble for **yes** or **no**.* (yes)

- *Point to box 4. Why do omnivores have both pointy and flat teeth?* (so they can eat both meat and plants) *Is this boy an **omnivore**? Fill in the answer bubble for **yes** or **no**.* (yes)

Day 2 activity

Life Science

- Understand that people, plants, and animals are living things with basic needs
- Infer what animals eat from the shapes of their teeth

Literacy

Oral Language Development

- Respond orally to simple questions

Comprehension

- Recall details
- Make inferences and draw conclusions

Developing the Concept

To introduce the activity, review the definitions of **carnivore**, **herbivore**, and **omnivore**. Say:

In our story, we learned that the dog was a carnivore, the pony was an herbivore, and the boy was an omnivore. Now let's learn about some other animals.

Distribute the Day 3 activity. Say:

- *Look at number 1. A horse is an **herbivore**. Does it eat meat, plants, or both?* (plants) *Which of these foods does a horse eat?* (hay, grass) *Draw a line under each one.*

- *Look at number 2. A lion is a **carnivore**. A carnivore eats meat or other animals. Which of these does a lion eat?* (zebra) *Draw a line under the zebra.*

- *Look at number 3. A wolf is a **carnivore**. What kind of food does it eat?* (meat) *Which of these might a wolf eat?* (chicken) *Draw a line under the chicken.*

- *Look at number 4. A giraffe is an **herbivore**. Which of these does it eat?* (leaves) *Draw a line under the leaves.*

- *Look at number 5. A grizzly bear is an **omnivore**. Does it eat meat, plants, or both?* (both) *Draw a line under everything it eats.*

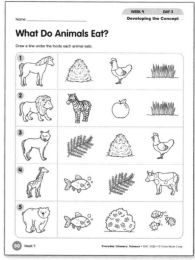

Day 3 activity

Life Science

• Understand that people, plants, and animals are living things with basic needs

• Infer what animals eat from the shapes of their teeth

Literacy

Oral Language Development

• Respond orally to simple questions

• Use new vocabulary

Comprehension

• Recall details

Extending the Concept

Introduce the Day 4 activity by saying:

You can tell what kind of food an animal eats by the shape of its teeth. What kind of teeth do meat eaters have? (sharp, pointed) What kind of teeth do plant eaters have? (flat, wide)

Distribute the Day 4 activity. Say:

• *Read the words in the box: **meat, plants**. Picture 1 shows a cat. What do its teeth look like? (sharp, pointed) Read the sentence with me: **A cat eats _____**. Write the word that completes the sentence. (meat)*

• *Picture 2 shows a deer. What do its teeth look like? (flat, wide) Read with me: **A deer eats _____**. Complete the sentence. (plants)*

• *Picture 3 shows a cow. What do its teeth look like? (flat, wide) Read with me: **A cow eats _____**. Complete the sentence. (plants)*

• *Picture 4 shows a wolf. What do its teeth look like? (sharp, pointed) Read with me: **A wolf eats _____**. Complete the sentence. (meat)*

Day 4 activity

Home–School Connection p. 82

Spanish version available (see p. 2)

Hands-on Science Activity

Reinforce this week's science concept with the following hands-on activity:

Materials: staple removers, flat rocks, rubber or leather scraps, beef jerky, pink erasers, uninflated balloons, leaves, grass, shredded paper, seeds

Activity: Introduce the activity by saying:

• *You learned that animals have different kinds of teeth. Flat, wide teeth are made for eating plants. Imagine that these flat rocks are the teeth of an **herbivore**.*

• *Sharp, pointy teeth are made for eating meat. Imagine that the staple removers are the sharp, pointy teeth of a **carnivore**.*

Have small groups of students explore how the staple remover teeth are best suited for tearing into or gripping the rubber scraps, beef jerky, pink erasers, and balloons.

Then have them use the flat rocks to represent the top and bottom teeth of an herbivore. Have students grind leaves, grass, shredded paper, and seeds, just as an herbivore would.

Name _____

What Do Animals Eat?

Name _____

What Do Animals Eat?

Listen. Fill in the circle for **yes** or **no**.

1 O yes   O no

2 O yes   O no

3 O yes   O no

4 O yes   O no

Name _____

What Do Animals Eat?

Draw a line under the foods each animal eats.

Name _____

What Do Animals Eat?

Write a word from the box to complete each sentence.

meat   plants

1

A cat eats _____ .

2

A deer eats _____ .

3

A cow eats _____ .

4

A wolf eats _____ .

Name _____

What I Learned

What to Do

Have your child look at the picture. Talk about the food that each animal eats. Have your child describe the teeth of each animal. Ask: *What kind of teeth do carnivores have?* (sharp, pointed) *What kind do herbivores have?* (flat, wide) *What kind do omnivores have?* (both) Then have your child color the picture.

Science Concept: Animals eat plants or other animals for food.

To Parents

This week your child learned about carnivores, herbivores, and omnivores.

What to Do Next

Help your child examine his or her own teeth in a mirror. Discuss the different shapes of teeth that people have (sharp, pointed, flat, wide). Then ask, *What types of foods do people eat? How do the different shapes of their teeth help them eat?*

Everyday Literacy: Science • EMC 5026 • © Evan-Moor Corp.

WEEK 10

Concept

Plants are living things that need water, sunlight, and air.

Looking at Leaves

Science Objective:

To help students understand that different trees have many different kinds of leaves and that leaves make food from water, sunlight, and air

Science Vocabulary:

air, edge, food, leaf, part, shape, size, stem, sunlight, tip, vein, water

Day 1
SKILLS

Life Science

• Understand that people, plants, and animals are living things with basic needs

• Understand that green leaves make food from sunlight

• Understand that leaves have parts

Literacy

Oral Language Development

• Respond orally to simple questions

Comprehension

• Recall details

• Make connections using illustrations, prior knowledge, or real-life experiences

• Answer questions about key details in a text read aloud

Introducing the Concept

Beforehand, collect a variety of leaves (or images of leaves) to display. Ask:

• *Are all these leaves from the same tree?* (no) *How do you know?* (Leaves from the same tree would look alike.)

• *These leaves are alike in some ways and different in others. One way they are alike is that they all have the same basic parts.* Point to each part as you name it: *stem, vein, edge, tip. How are these leaves different?* (different sizes, shapes, colors) *There is another way that leaves are alike. They all make food for their tree.*

Listening to the Story

Direct students' attention to the Day 1 activity page. Say: *Listen and look at the picture as I read a story about a boy who collects leaves.*

Anthony's class was learning about leaves. They had just come back from a leaf walk, and Anthony was gluing leaves into his tree book. As he worked, his teacher explained: "Trees have leaves of different sizes and shapes. Some are flat and wide; some are spiky and thin. You can tell what tree a leaf came from by looking at its shape and edges. Leaves are important to a tree because they make food for the tree. They make food from water, sunlight, and air. Leaves grow on the sides and tips of tree branches, so they get lots of sunshine. Can you guess what they give us? Shade!"

Confirming Understanding

Reinforce the science concept by asking students questions about the story. Ask:

• *Why are leaves important to a tree?* (They make food for the tree.) *Make a green dot on the tree.*

• *How are Anthony's leaves different?* (sizes, shapes, edges) *Use red to circle any two leaves that are **different** from each other.*

• *Are Anthony's leaves all from the same kind of tree?* (no) *How do you know?* (They have different shapes and edges.) *Color the two leaves that could be from the **same** kind of tree.*

Day 1 picture

Life Science

• Understand that people, plants, and animals are living things with basic needs

• Understand that green leaves make food from sunlight

Literacy

Oral Language Development

• Respond orally to simple questions

Comprehension

• Recall details

• Make connections using illustrations, prior knowledge, or real-life experiences

Reinforcing the Concept

Reread the Day 1 story. Then reinforce this week's science concept by guiding a discussion about the story. Ask:

Can leaves have different shapes, edges, and sizes? (yes) Why are leaves important to a tree? (They make food for their tree.)

Distribute the Day 2 activity. Say:

• *Point to box 1. Are these leaves from the same kind of tree? Fill in the answer bubble for* **yes** *or* **no**. *(no) How do you know? (They have different shapes.)*

• *Point to box 2. Do leaves grow on the sides and tips of tree branches? Fill in the answer bubble for* **yes** *or* **no**. *(yes)*

• *Point to box 3. Are these leaves from the same kind of tree? Fill in the answer bubble for* **yes** *or* **no**. *(yes)*

• *Point to box 4. Does this picture show something that helps the leaves make food for the tree? Fill in the answer bubble for* **yes** *or* **no**. *(yes) What is it? (sunlight)*

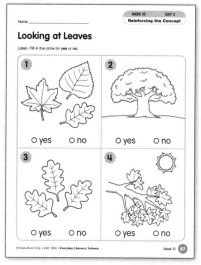

Day 2 activity

Life Science

• Understand that green leaves make food from sunlight

• Understand that leaves have parts

Literacy

Oral Language Development

• Use new vocabulary

Comprehension

• Make connections using illustrations, prior knowledge, or real-life experiences

Applying the Concept

Introduce the activity by reviewing the science concept. Say:

Different trees have different kinds of leaves, but all leaves make food from water, sunlight, and air.

Distribute the Day 3 activity. Say:

• *Point to number 1. This word is* **sun**. *Let's read it together:* **sun**. *Leaves take in light from the sun. Draw a line from the word* **sun** *to the picture of the sun.*

• *Point to number 2. This word is* **tree**. *Let's read it together:* **tree**. *Trees have leaves of different shapes and sizes. Draw a line from the word* **tree** *to the picture of the tree.*

• *Point to number 3. This word is* **leaf**. *Let's read it together:* **leaf**. *A leaf grows on a tree. Draw a line from the word* **leaf** *to the picture of the leaf.*

• *Think about the parts of a leaf:* **stem**, **vein**, **edge**, **tip**. *Draw a picture of a leaf at the bottom of the page. Remember to include all the parts.*

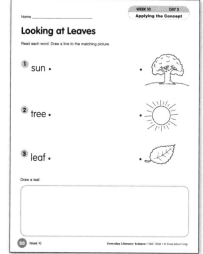

Day 3 activity

Life Science

• Understand that people, plants, and animals are living things with basic needs

• Understand that leaves have parts

Literacy

Oral Language Development

• Use new vocabulary

• Respond orally to simple questions

Comprehension

• Recall details

• Make connections using illustrations, prior knowledge, or real-life experiences

Extending the Concept

To introduce the activity, guide a discussion that helps students recall the Day 1 story. Say:

*In our story, Anthony collected leaves. How are leaves different from each other? (shapes, edges, sizes, colors) Leaves are different, but they are also the same. They all have the same four parts: **stem**, **vein**, **edge**, **tip**.*

Distribute the Day 4 activity. Say:

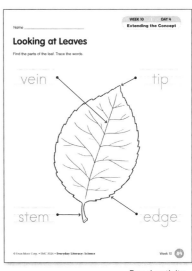

Day 4 activity

• *Look at the leaf. The part that attaches the leaf to the branch is called the **stem**. Point to the stem. Follow the line from the stem to the word **stem**. Let's read it: **stem**. Trace the word **stem**.*

• *The **vein** is like the skeleton of the leaf. Point to the main vein running down the center of the leaf. Notice the smaller veins. Follow the line from the vein to the word **vein**. Let's read it: **vein**. Trace the word **vein**.*

• *The **edge** of the leaf is its outline. Run your finger around the edge of the leaf. Follow the line to the word **edge**. Let's read it: **edge**. Trace the word **edge**.*

• *The **tip** is the top part. Point to the tip of the leaf. Follow the line to the word **tip**. Let's read it: **tip**. Trace the word **tip**.*

Home–School Connection p. 90
Spanish version available (see p. 2)

Hands-on Science Activity

Reinforce this week's science concept with the following hands-on activity:

Materials: one leaf per student, hand lenses, paper, crayons

Preparation: Flatten the leaves a few days in advance by placing them between sheets of paper and stacking books on top of them.

Activity: Distribute a leaf to each student. Guide their observations with the following questions:

• *Touch your leaf. Is it rough or smooth?*

• *Smell your leaf. What does it smell like?*

• *Listen to your leaf. What sounds can you make with it?*

• *Look at your leaf with a hand lens. Can you find veins, bumps, holes, or jagged edges? Where is the tip? Can you hold it by the stem?*

Have students place their leaf under the paper, bumpy side up, and use the side of a crayon to make a rubbing of it. Have students identify and label the four parts of the leaf: **stem**, **vein**, **edge**, **tip**.

Name _____

Looking at Leaves

Name _____

Looking at Leaves

Listen. Fill in the circle for **yes** or **no**.

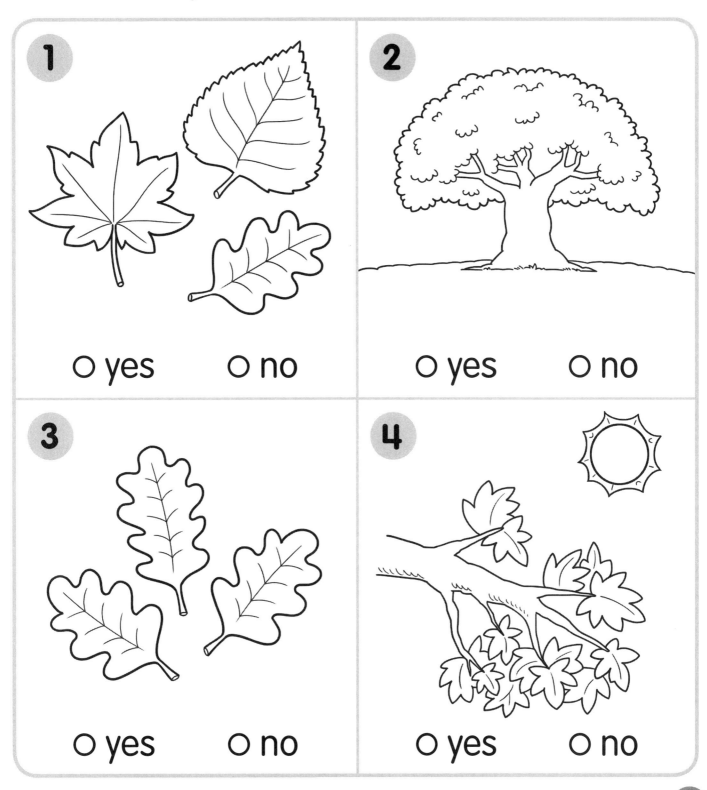

Name _____

Looking at Leaves

Read each word. Draw a line to the matching picture.

1 sun •

2 tree •

3 leaf •

Draw a leaf.

Name _____

Looking at Leaves

Find the parts of the leaf. Trace the words.

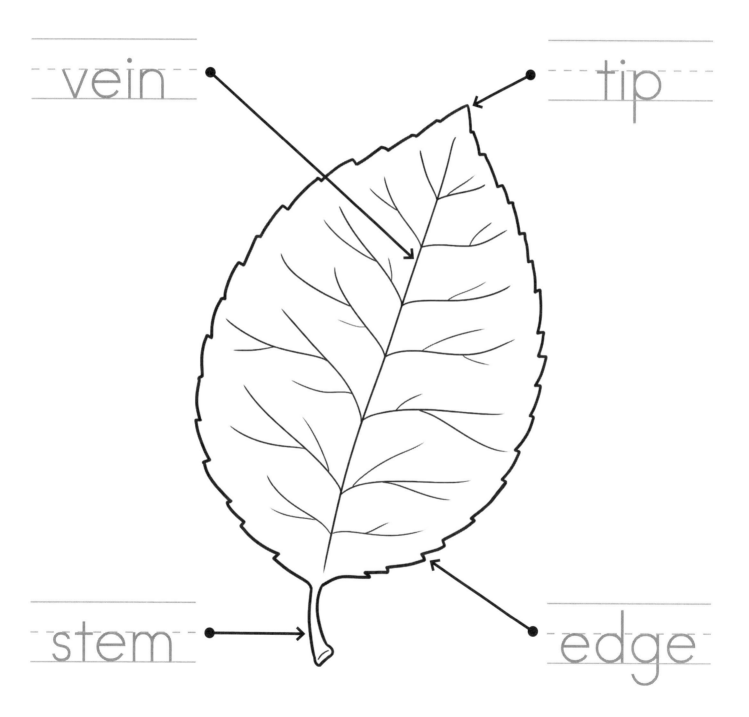

vein

tip

stem

edge

Name _____

What I Learned

What to Do
Have your child look at the picture below. Read the names of the leaves on the poster in the picture to your child. Then have your child point out which of the boy's leaves match a leaf on the poster.

WEEK 10

Home–School Connection

Science Concept: Plants are living things that need water, air, and sunlight.

To Parents
This week your child learned that different trees have a variety of leaves.

What to Do Next
Take a discovery walk with your child. Look for leaves from various trees. Have your child tell you how they are alike and different in shape, size, color, edges, veins, and so on.

Everyday Literacy: Science • EMC 5026 • © Evan-Moor Corp.

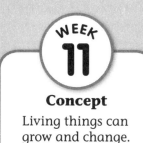

WEEK 11

Concept
Living things can grow and change.

Growing and Changing

Science Objective:
To help students understand that living things grow and change

Science Vocabulary:
butterfly, caterpillar, chrysalis, egg, pupa

Day 1 SKILLS

Life Science
- Understand that people, plants, and animals are living things with basic needs
- Recognize that animals have life cycles
- Understand that living things grow and change

Literacy

Oral Language Development
- Respond orally to simple questions

Comprehension
- Recall details
- Make connections using illustrations, prior knowledge, or real-life experiences
- Answer questions about key details in a text read aloud
- Make inferences and draw conclusions

Introducing the Concept

Activate prior knowledge about how living things grow and change. Ask:

- *How have you grown since you were a baby?* (students respond) *How have you changed?* (students respond)
- *Have you ever seen a caterpillar or butterfly? Where?* (students respond) *A butterfly grows in four stages. First, it is an* **egg***. Second, a* **caterpillar** *hatches and grows. Third, it forms a* **chrysalis** *and turns into a* **pupa***. Fourth, the pupa grows into a* **butterfly***.*

Listening to the Story

Distribute the Day 1 activity page. Say: *Listen and look at the picture as I read a story about a girl who finds a caterpillar.*

Chloe found a tiny creature crawling on a bush. Chloe's mom gave her a container for it. Mom said the creature was a caterpillar. It had hatched from an egg on a leaf. The caterpillar's mother had laid the egg there so the caterpillar would have leaves to eat. Chloe got some leaves and twigs from the bush and put them in the caterpillar's container. For days, the caterpillar grew and grew. Then one day it was gone, but there was a small sack hanging from a twig. The caterpillar had made a **chrysalis** *around itself! Inside, it had turned itself into a* **pupa** *and was slowly changing. Weeks later, Chloe saw the chrysalis break open. Something was coming out. She watched the creature unfold its wings and flutter into the air. It was a beautiful butterfly!*

Confirming Understanding

Reinforce the science concept by asking students questions about the story. Ask:

- *What laid an egg on a leaf?* (butterfly) *Circle the leaf and egg.*
- *What hatched from the egg?* (caterpillar) *Make a dot on the caterpillar.*
- *What was hanging from the twig during the pupa stage?* (chrysalis) *Point to the chrysalis.*
- *What came out of the chrysalis?* (butterfly) *Make an* **X** *on the butterfly.*

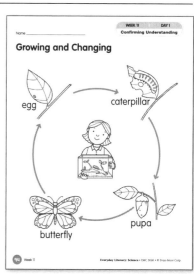

Day 1 picture

Life Science

- Understand that people, plants, and animals are living things with basic needs
- Recognize that animals have life cycles
- Understand that living things grow and change

Literacy

Oral Language Development

- Respond orally to simple questions

Comprehension

- Make connections using illustrations, prior knowledge, or real-life experiences
- Answer questions about key details in a text read aloud

Reinforcing the Concept

Reread the Day 1 story. Then reinforce this week's science concept by guiding a discussion about the story. Say:

Our story was about a girl who found a tiny creature. What was it? (caterpillar) What did it become? (pupa, then butterfly)

Distribute the Day 2 activity. Say:

- *Point to box 1. These eggs are on the underside of a leaf. Does a butterfly lay its eggs on a leaf? Fill in the answer bubble for* **yes** *or* **no**. *(yes) Why is that a good place? (A leaf provides food and protection for a caterpillar.)*

- *Point to box 2. A caterpillar hatches from a butterfly egg. Does this picture show a caterpillar? Fill in the answer bubble for* **yes** *or* **no**. *(yes) What does a caterpillar do? (crawls, eats, and grows)*

- *Point to box 3. Was Chloe's caterpillar really gone in the story? (no) Where was it? (It had become a pupa hooked onto a twig.) Does this picture show a pupa? Fill in the answer bubble for* **yes** *or* **no**. *(yes)*

- *Point to box 4. Does this picture show a caterpillar? Fill in the answer bubble for* **yes** *or* **no**. *(no) What has the caterpillar become? (butterfly)*

Day 2 activity

Life Science

- Understand that people, plants, and animals are living things with basic needs
- Recognize that animals have life cycles
- Understand that living things grow and change

Literacy

Comprehension

- Recall details
- Make connections using illustrations, prior knowledge, or real-life experiences

Developing the Concept

Introduce the activity by saying:

We have learned how a butterfly grows in four stages. It looks different at each stage. Not all animals change that much as they grow. Some of their parts change and some stay the same.

Distribute the Day 3 activity. Say:

- *Look at row 1. What does a puppy grow into? (a dog) How does a puppy change? (gets bigger; acts differently) Find the word* **puppy** *and trace it. Then find the word* **dog** *and trace it.*

- *Look at row 2. A baby cat, or kitten, is tiny and playful. How will it grow and change? (students respond) What does a kitten have that it will still have when it is a cat? (tail, whiskers, pointy ears, fur, etc.) Find the word* **kitten** *and trace it. Then find the word* **cat** *and trace it.*

- *Look at row 3. A baby rooster, or chick, hatches from an egg. How will the chick grow and change? (students respond) What will stay the same about the chick? (feathers, wings, two legs, beak, etc.) What will be different? (color, size, crowing) Find the word* **chick** *and trace it. Then find the word* **rooster** *and trace it.*

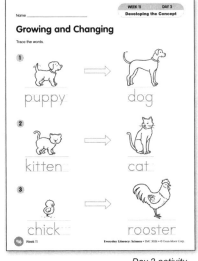

Day 3 activity

Day 4
SKILLS

Life Science
- Understand that people, plants, and animals are living things with basic needs
- Recognize that animals have life cycles
- Understand that living things grow and change

Literacy

Oral Language Development
- Respond orally to simple questions
- Use new vocabulary

Comprehension
- Make connections using illustrations, prior knowledge, or real-life experiences
- Make inferences and draw conclusions

Extending the Concept

Extend the science concept to introduce another animal that undergoes a complete transformation during its life cycle:

We learned about how a butterfly goes through four completely different stages as it grows. A frog is another animal that does this. Review the life cycle of a frog with students. (starts as an egg, hatches into a tadpole, grows legs and loses tail, finally becomes frog)

Distribute the Day 4 activity. Say: *Let's think about how butterflies and frogs grow.*

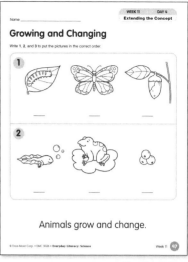

Day 4 activity

- *Point to row 1. Which picture shows what happens first?* (caterpillar) *Write **1** below that picture. What happens second?* (pupa) *Write **2** below that picture. What happens last?* (butterfly) *Write **3** below that picture.*

- *Point to row 2. Which picture shows what happens first?* (eggs) *Write **1** below that picture. What happens second?* (tadpole) *Write **2** below that picture. What happens last?* (frog) *Write **3** below that picture.*

- *Let's read the sentence at the bottom:* **Animals grow and change.** *Point to the last word.* (change) *Tell about the changes a butterfly goes through. Tell about the changes a frog goes through.* (students respond) *How are these changes different from the changes a puppy goes through?* (A puppy looks basically the same. A butterfly does not look like a caterpillar, and a frog does not look like a tadpole.)

Day 5
SKILLS

Life Science
- Recognize that animals have life cycles
- Understand that living things grow and change

Home–School Connection p. 98
Spanish version available (see p. 2)

Hands-on Science Activity

Reinforce this week's science concept with the following hands-on activity:

Materials: paper plates; leaves and twigs cut from construction paper; glue; bowtie, rotini, and shell pasta shapes; pearl barley; black pipe cleaners

Preparation: Display the words **egg**, **caterpillar**, **pupa**, and **butterfly**. Provide small groups with materials to share.

Activity: Have students use pasta shapes to represent the stages of a butterfly's growth. First, have students divide their plates into four sections, one for each life-cycle stage. Then instruct students to do the following: Glue pearl barley onto a construction paper leaf for the egg stage. The next stage features a rotini pasta caterpillar glued onto another paper leaf. Glue a pasta shell onto a paper twig for the pupa stage. Make a butterfly body and antennas out of pipe cleaners and use bowtie pasta wings. Have students finish their butterfly cycles by labeling each stage: **egg**, **caterpillar**, **pupa**, **butterfly**.

Name _____

Growing and Changing

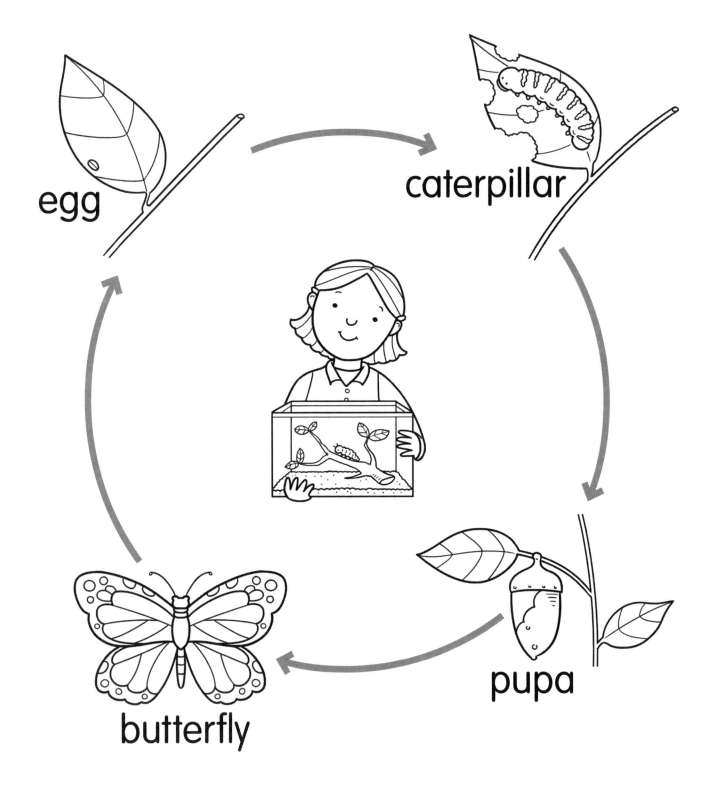

egg

caterpillar

pupa

butterfly

Name _____

Growing and Changing

Listen. Fill in the circle for **yes** or **no**.

1

○ yes   ○ no

2

○ yes   ○ no

3

○ yes   ○ no

4

○ yes   ○ no

Name _____

Growing and Changing

Trace the words.

1

 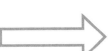 

puppy

dog

2

kitten

cat

3

chick

rooster

Name _____

Growing and Changing

Write **1**, **2**, and **3** to put the pictures in the correct order.

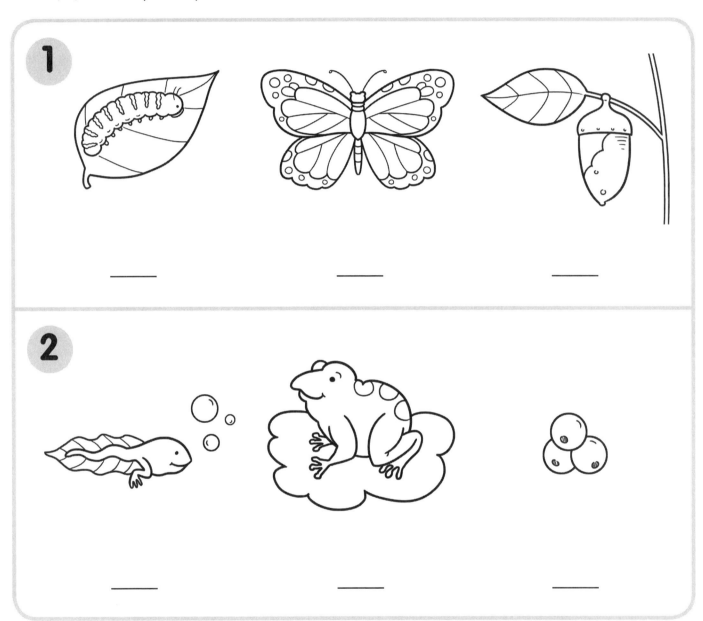

Animals grow and change.

Name _____

What I Learned

What to Do
Look at the picture below with your child. Talk about how an egg grows and changes into a butterfly. Then have your child color the picture.

WEEK 11

Home–School Connection

Science Concept: Living things can grow and change.

To Parents
This week your child learned about different ways that animals grow and change.

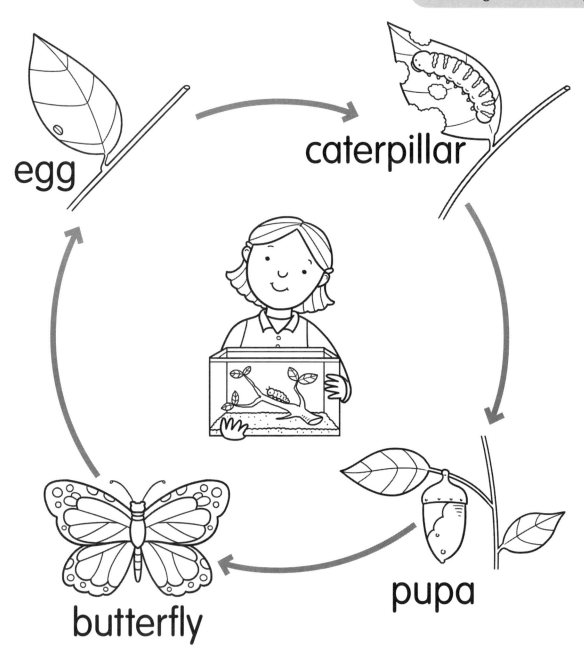

egg

caterpillar

pupa

butterfly

What to Do Next
Look at your child's baby pictures together and discuss how he or she has grown and changed.

Everyday Literacy: Science • EMC 5026 • © Evan-Moor Corp.

Concept

Animals respond to seasonal changes in a variety of ways.

Animals in Winter

Science Objective:
To help students understand that animals survive winter by migrating, hibernating, or staying in place

Science Vocabulary:
den, hibernate, migrate, store, survive, winter

Day 1 SKILLS

Life Science
- Understand that people, plants, and animals are living things with basic needs
- Recognize changes in appearance that animals go through as seasons change
- Understand that some animal behaviors are influenced by environmental conditions

Literacy

Oral Language Development
- Respond orally to simple questions

Comprehension
- Make connections using illustrations, prior knowledge, or real-life experiences
- Answer questions about key details in a text read aloud
- Make inferences and draw conclusions

Introducing the Concept

Brainstorm how people survive during cold winters (stay inside; dress warmly; build fires). Then say: *Many animals have ways to survive during winter, too.*

- *Some animals survive by traveling to warmer places to find food. They* **migrate***. For example, birds migrate. Do you know of any other animals that migrate?* (fish, Monarch butterflies, etc.)

- *Other animals, like mice, survive by collecting and storing food all fall to eat during winter. Or they might eat whatever they can find near them. A deer will eat bark and twigs during winter, for example. Do you know of any other animals that stay around all winter?* (rabbits, squirrels, etc.)

Listening to the Story

Distribute the Day 1 activity page. Say: *Listen and look at the picture as I read a story about a squirrel getting ready for winter.*

---

*One fall day, Joey and Uncle Matt were strolling in the park when they saw a squirrel scamper down a tree. It had an acorn in its mouth. The squirrel dug a hole near the tree and dropped the acorn into it. "That squirrel is storing food for the winter," said Uncle Matt. "Its winter den is in that tree. The squirrel will live there all winter." Just then, a flock of geese honked noisily overhead. "But those geese aren't sticking around this winter," laughed Joey. "They're heading south to someplace warmer." Joey and Uncle Matt waved goodbye as the geese formed a giant **V** in the sky and flew off.*

Confirming Understanding

Reinforce the science concept by asking questions about the story. Ask:

- *Why did the squirrel drop an acorn into the hole?* (to store it for winter) *Circle the acorn.*

- *Where will the squirrel live during winter?* (the den in the tree) *Make an **X** on the squirrel's den.*

- *Will the geese stay around, just like the squirrel?* (no) *What will they do?* (migrate, or fly south) *Trace the geese's giant **V** shape in the sky.*

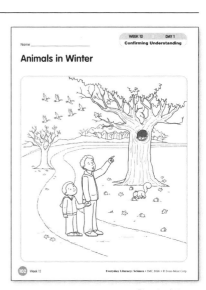

Day 1 picture

Day 2
SKILLS

Life Science
- Understand that people, plants, and animals are living things with basic needs
- Understand that some animal behaviors are influenced by environmental conditions

Literacy

Oral Language Development
- Respond orally to simple questions

Comprehension
- Recall details
- Make connections using illustrations, prior knowledge, or real-life experiences
- Answer questions about key details in a text read aloud
- Make inferences and draw conclusions

Reinforcing the Concept

Reread the Day 1 story. Reinforce this week's science concept by discussing the story. Say:

Our story is about a squirrel getting ready for winter and some geese flying south.

- *Why does a squirrel bury acorns in fall?* (to store them for winter)
- *Why do geese migrate?* (to go where there is food and warmer weather)

Distribute the Day 2 activity. Say:

- *Point to box 1. Some animals migrate to warmer places during the winter. Does a squirrel migrate? Fill in the answer bubble for **yes** or **no**.* (no) *Where does a squirrel stay during winter?* (in a den)
- *Point to box 2. Squirrels make a den to stay warm and dry on cold days. Does this picture show a squirrel's den? Fill in the answer bubble for **yes** or **no**.* (yes) *Where is the squirrel's den?* (hole in tree)
- *Point to box 3. What is the squirrel doing?* (putting acorns in the ground) *Will the squirrel come back for the acorns in the winter? Fill in the answer bubble for **yes** or **no**.* (yes)
- *Point to box 4. Do squirrels and geese spend the winter in the same way? Fill in the answer bubble for **yes** or **no**.* (no) *What are the geese doing in this picture?* (migrating, or flying south)

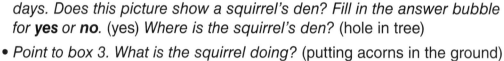

Day 2 activity

Day 3
SKILLS

Life Science
- Understand that people, plants, and animals are living things with basic needs
- Understand that some animal behaviors are influenced by environmental conditions

Literacy

Oral Language Development
- Respond orally to simple questions

Comprehension
- Make connections using illustrations, prior knowledge, or real-life experiences
- Make inferences and draw conclusions

Applying the Concept

Distribute the Day 3 activity. Then introduce the activity by reviewing the science concept. Ask:

How do animals survive during the winter? (Some animals migrate, and some stay in place.) *This picture shows animals who do something else. They **hibernate**.*

- *Find the bear. It is in a den. In the fall, a bear grows thicker fur and eats more to build up its body fat. Then it goes into a deep sleep and stays that way all winter. A bear **hibernates**. Make a circle around the bear.*
- *Bats hibernate, too. They hang upside down in a cave. Find the bats in this picture. Make an **X** on each bat.*
- *A groundhog also hibernates, but it sleeps in a hole underground. Find the groundhog. Draw a line under the groundhog.*
- *The bear, bats, and groundhog will be in a deep sleep until spring. They are **hibernating**. Can you find two other animals that are <u>not</u> hibernating?* (squirrel and rabbit) *Make a dot on the squirrel and the rabbit.*

Day 3 activity

100 Week 12

Everyday Literacy: Science • EMC 5026 • © Evan-Moor Corp.

Day 4
SKILLS

Life Science
- Understand that people, plants, and animals are living things with basic needs
- Understand that some animal behaviors are influenced by environmental conditions

Literacy

Oral Language Development
- Respond orally to simple questions
- Use new vocabulary

Comprehension
- Make connections using illustrations, prior knowledge, or real-life experiences
- Make inferences and draw conclusions

Applying the Concept

Distribute the Day 4 activity and review:

Animals survive the winter by migrating, hibernating, or staying in place.

- *Point to the first word: **migrate**. Let's see which animals are migrating. The first picture shows geese flying south for the winter. Are the geese **migrating**?* (yes) *Circle the geese.*

Continue the process for the squirrel (does not migrate) and the Monarch butterflies (do migrate).

- *Point to the second word: **hibernate**. Let's see which animals are hibernating. What does the first picture show?* (sleeping bear) *Is this bear **hibernating**?* (yes) *Circle the bear.*

Continue the process for the robin (does not hibernate) and the groundhog (does hibernate).

- *Point to the next set of words: **stay in place**. Let's see which animals stay in place. What does the first picture show?* (mouse) *Does it store food for the winter and **stay in place**?* (yes) *Circle the mouse.*

Continue the process for the squirrel and the rabbit (both stay in place).

Day 4 activity

Day 5
SKILLS

Life Science
- Understand that people, plants, and animals are living things with basic needs
- Understand that some animal behaviors are influenced by environmental conditions

Scientific Thinking & Inquiry
- Sort objects according to common characteristics

Home–School Connection p. 106
Spanish version available (see p. 2)

Hands-on Science Activity

Reinforce this week's science concept with the following hands-on activity:

Materials: bedsheets or large towels

Preparation: Drape bedsheets over furniture to create winter "dens" for students to "hibernate" in.

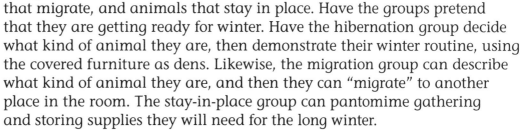

Activity: Divide the class into three groups: animals that hibernate, animals that migrate, and animals that stay in place. Have the groups pretend that they are getting ready for winter. Have the hibernation group decide what kind of animal they are, then demonstrate their winter routine, using the covered furniture as dens. Likewise, the migration group can describe what kind of animal they are, and then they can "migrate" to another place in the room. The stay-in-place group can pantomime gathering and storing supplies they will need for the long winter.

Have each group tell the class how they survived during winter. Prompt students with questions such as, *What did you eat? Where did you sleep? How did you stay warm?*

Name _____

Animals in Winter

Name _____

Animals in Winter

Listen. Fill in the circle for **yes** or **no**.

1

○ yes   ○ no

2

○ yes   ○ no

3

○ yes   ○ no

4

○ yes   ○ no

Name _____

Animals in Winter

Listen. Circle the animals to show what they do in winter.

Everyday Literacy: Science • EMC 5026 • © Evan-Moor Corp.

Animals in Winter

Listen. Circle the correct animals.

 migrate

 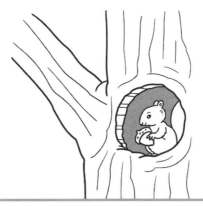 

2 **hibernate**

  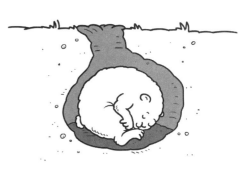

3 **stay in place**

Name _____

What I Learned

What to Do

Have your child look at the picture below. Ask him or her to point to and name the animals. Ask: *Which animal's home is empty?* (bird's nest) Then have your child tell you what each animal does to survive during winter: sleeps (hibernates), moves to a warmer place (migrates), or stays in place.

Science Concept: Animals respond to seasonal changes in a variety of ways.

To Parents

This week your child learned that animals hibernate, migrate, or stay in place.

What to Do Next

Have your child role-play different animals, showing what they do during winter to survive.

Everyday Literacy: Science • EMC 5026 • © Evan-Moor Corp.

Animals and Their Babies

Science Objective:
To help students understand that many baby animals look like their parents

Science Vocabulary:
bear, calf, chick, chicken, cow, cub, deer, duck, duckling, fawn, foal, goat, hen, horse, kid, pig, piglet, resemble

Day 1
SKILLS

Life Science
- Understand that living things grow and change
- Describe ways in which animals closely resemble their parents in appearance

Literacy

Oral Language Development
- Respond orally to simple questions

Comprehension
- Make connections using illustrations, prior knowledge, or real-life experiences
- Answer questions about key details in a text read aloud
- Make inferences and draw conclusions

Introducing the Concept

Before the lesson, on letter-size cardstock, prepare and display labeled pictures of the animals listed above. These cards will be used for an activity at the end of the week. Then activate students' prior knowledge by asking:

- *What baby animals have you seen?* (students respond)
- *What did the baby animals look like? How were they the same as their parents?* (e.g., legs, eyes, ears, nose, fur, feathers, tail, feet or paws) *Most often, baby animals* **resemble***, or look like, their parents.*

Listening to the Story

Distribute the Day 1 activity page. Say: *Listen and look at the picture as I read a story about a girl who learns about animals and their babies.*

At school, Lily played a computer game called "Where's My Mama?" It was fun. First, Lily saw a big picture of a cub on the computer screen. Then she looked at three small pictures of grown-up animals: a deer, a horse, and a bear. Which one should she choose? The bear's eyes, ears, nose, legs, paws, tail, and fur looked like the cub's. Lily clicked on the picture of the bear. Correct! A cub becomes a bear when it grows up. Lily played the rest of the game. By the time she had finished, she had learned that baby animals usually look a lot like their parents. Lily matched ten out of ten babies and mamas correctly!

Confirming Understanding

Reinforce the science concept by asking students questions about the story. Ask:

- *What does a cub grow up to be?* (bear) *Draw a line from the cub to the bear.*
- *Does a cub look like its parents?* (yes) *In what way?* (same eyes, ears, nose, legs, paws, tail, fur) *Circle the bears' faces.*
- *Find the deer in the picture. A baby deer is called a* **fawn***. Does a* **fawn** *look like a bear?* (no) *Make an* **X** *on the deer.*
- *A baby horse is called a* **foal***. Does a* **foal** *look like a bear?* (no) *Make an* **X** *on the horse.*

Day 1 picture

Day 2 SKILLS

Life Science
- Understand that living things grow and change
- Describe ways in which animals closely resemble their parents in appearance

Literacy

Oral Language Development
- Respond orally to simple questions

Comprehension
- Recall details
- Make connections using illustrations, prior knowledge, or real-life experiences
- Answer questions about key details in a text read aloud
- Make inferences and draw conclusions

Reinforcing the Concept

Reread the Day 1 story. Then reinforce this week's science concept by guiding a discussion about the story. Say:

In our story, Lily looked at animal pictures. What did she learn? (Baby animals usually look like their parents.)

Distribute the Day 2 activity. Say:

- *Point to box 1. It shows an elephant and a lion cub. Do they look like each other?* (no) *How are they different?* (students respond) *Is the elephant the cub's mother? Fill in the answer bubble for **yes** or **no**.* (no)

- *Look at box 2. It shows a cow and a calf. Do they look like each other?* (yes) *How are they the same?* (students respond) *Is the cow the calf's mother? Fill in the answer bubble for **yes** or **no**.* (yes)

- *Look at box 3. It shows a pig and a piglet. Do they look like each other?* (yes) *How are they the same?* (students respond) *Is the pig the piglet's mother? Fill in the answer bubble for **yes** or **no**.* (yes)

- *Look at box 4. It shows a duckling and a rabbit. Do they look like each other?* (no) *How are they different?* (students respond) *Is the rabbit the duckling's mother? Fill in the answer bubble for **yes** or **no**.* (no)

Day 2 activity

Day 3 SKILLS

Life Science
- Understand that living things grow and change

Literacy

Oral Language Development
- Use new vocabulary

Comprehension
- Make connections using illustrations, prior knowledge, or real-life experiences

Developing the Concept

Distribute the Day 3 activity. Then introduce the activity by reviewing:

Most baby animals look like their parents. Let's read and write the names of some babies and match them to their pictures.

- *Look at number 1. A baby bear is a **cub**. Let's read the word together: **cub**. Trace the letters. Draw a line to the cub and its parent. Circle the cub.*

- *Look at number 2. A baby cow is called a **calf**. Let's read the word together: **calf**. Trace the letters. Draw a line to the calf and its parent. Circle the calf.*

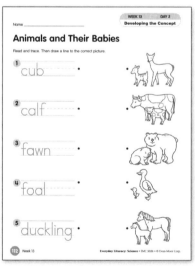

Day 3 activity

- *Look at number 3. A baby deer is called a **fawn**. Let's read the word together: **fawn**. Trace the letters. Draw a line to the fawn and its parent. Circle the fawn.*

- *Look at number 4. A baby horse is a **foal**. Let's read the word: **foal**. Trace the letters. Draw a line to the foal and its parent. Circle the foal.*

- *Look at number 5. A baby duck is a **duckling**. Let's read the word together: **duckling**. Trace the letters. Draw a line to the duckling and its parent. Circle the duckling.*

Everyday Literacy: Science • EMC 5026 • © Evan-Moor Corp.

Life Science

• Understand that living things grow and change

Literacy

Oral Language Development

• Respond orally to simple questions

Comprehension

• Make connections using illustrations, prior knowledge, or real-life experiences

Applying the Concept

Distribute the Day 4 activity. Then introduce the activity by saying:

Day 4 activity

Baby animals grow and change. When animals grow up, they usually look like their parents.

- *Let's read the words in the gray box: **kid**, **cub**, **piglet**, **chick**. Look at row 1. The first picture shows a **kid**. Find the word **kid** in the gray box. Write it in the boxes. What does a kid grow up to be? (goat) Circle the picture of the goat. Let's read the word: **goat**.*

- *Look at row 2. The first picture shows a **chick**. Find the word **chick** and write it in the boxes. What does a chick grow up to be? (chicken) Circle the picture of the chicken. Let's read the word: **chicken**.*

- *Look at row 3. The first picture shows a **cub**. Find the word **cub** and write it in the boxes. What does a **cub** grow up to be? (bear) Circle the picture of the bear. Let's read the word: **bear**.*

- *Look at row 4. The first picture shows a **piglet**. Find the word **piglet** and write it in the boxes. What does a piglet grow up to be? (pig) Circle the picture of the pig. Let's read the word: **pig**.*

Life Science

• Understand that living things grow and change

Literacy

Oral Language Development

• Respond orally to simple questions

Comprehension

• Make connections using illustrations, prior knowledge, or real-life experiences

Home–School Connection p. 114
Spanish version available (see p. 2)

Hands-on Science Activity

Reinforce this week's science concept with the following hands-on activity:

Materials: labeled animal cards from Day 1

Activity: Distribute the animal cards, one per student. Have students hold their cards to their chests so as not to reveal their identity just yet.

At your signal, students should set off to find their mama or their baby, asking each other: "Are you my mama?" or "Are you my baby?" Students should compare their cards to determine if there is a match.

Reunited mothers and babies may stand to the side until everyone is paired up. In the end, have each pair show their cards and say the names of the animal's parent and baby.

Name _____

Animals and Their Babies

Everyday Literacy: Science • EMC 5026 • © Evan-Moor Corp.

Name _____

Animals and Their Babies

Listen. Fill in the circle for **yes** or **no**.

1
○ yes   ○ no

2
○ yes   ○ no

3
○ yes   ○ no

4
○ yes   ○ no

Name _____

Animals and Their Babies

Read and trace. Then draw a line to the correct picture.

1 cub •

2 calf •

3 fawn •

4 foal •

5 duckling •

Everyday Literacy: Science • EMC 5026 • © Evan-Moor Corp.

Name _____

Animals and Their Babies

Write the baby's name. Then circle the animal it becomes.

| kid | cub | piglet | chick |

1

goat    deer    horse

2

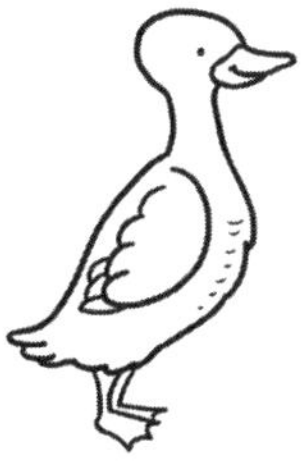

duck    pig    chicken

3

bear    rabbit    squirrel

4

cow    goat    pig

Name _____

What I Learned

What to Do
Have your child look at the pictures and match the baby animals with their parents. Read the names together. (fawn/deer; calf/cow; kid/goat; duckling/duck; foal/horse)

WEEK 13

Home–School Connection

Science Concept: Animals resemble their parents.

To Parents
This week your child learned that many baby animals look like their parents.

 •   •

 •   •

 •   •

 •   •

 •   •

What to Do Next
Have your child draw a picture of a baby animal he or she has seen.

Everyday Literacy: Science • EMC 5026 • © Evan-Moor Corp.

Concept
Living things have parts.

The Brain and Skull

Science Objective:
To help students learn the functions of the human brain and skull

Science Vocabulary:
bone, brain, control, helmet, protect, skull

Day 1
SKILLS

Life Science
• Understand that people are living things that have parts

Literacy

Oral Language Development
• Respond orally to simple questions

Comprehension
• Make connections using illustrations, prior knowledge, or real-life experiences
• Answer questions about key details in a text read aloud
• Make inferences and draw conclusions

Introducing the Concept

Explain that our brain tells our body how to move. Say:

• *Follow my instructions: Pat the top of your head with your hand. Make a funny face. Stand up. Sit down.*

• *Your brain controls everything you do, from breathing and blinking to running and playing. Your brain is inside your head.*

Listening to the Story

Distribute the Day 1 activity page. Say: *Listen and look at the picture as I read a story about Noah's brain.*

Noah's grandpa dropped him off at school and tapped him on the head. "Remember to use your brain today," he joked. Noah smiled. Of course he would use his brain! Grandpa had taught Noah that his brain is always working, even when he's asleep. Noah's brain controls everything his body does. Noah uses his brain to see, hear, touch, speak, and move. He uses it to learn and remember. Noah's brain even keeps his lungs breathing and his heart beating. Noah's brain is important. That's why it is inside his skull—thick, hard bone. The skull does a good job of protecting Noah's hardworking brain!

Confirming Understanding

Reinforce the science concept by asking students questions about the story. Ask:

• *What body part controls all of Noah's movements?* (brain) *Draw a line from Noah's head to his foot.*

• *What body part protects Noah's brain?* (skull) *Where is his skull?* (inside his head) *Draw a circle around Noah's head. Then tap your head to feel your own skull.*

• *What body parts do Noah and his grandpa use to listen and talk to each other?* (brain, ears, mouth) *Draw a line from Noah's head to Grandpa's head.*

Day 1 picture

Life Science

• Understand that people are living things that have parts

Literacy

Oral Language Development

• Respond orally to simple questions

Comprehension

• Recall details

• Make connections using illustrations, prior knowledge, or real-life experiences

Reinforcing the Concept

Reread the Day 1 story. Then reinforce this week's science concept by guiding a discussion about the story. Say:

In our story, Noah's brain helps him do many things. Where is his brain? (inside his skull, in his head)

Distribute the Day 2 activity. Say:

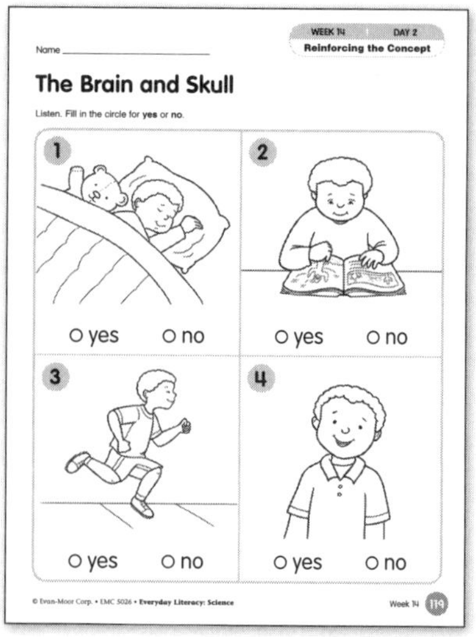

• *Point to box 1. What is Noah doing?* (sleeping) *Is his brain asleep, too? Fill in the answer bubble for **yes** or **no**.* (no) *Our brain is working even when we are asleep.*

• *Point to box 2. What is Noah doing?* (reading) *Is he using his brain to read? Fill in the answer bubble for **yes** or **no**.* (yes) *Our brain helps us read, write, learn, and remember.*

• *Point to box 3. What is Noah doing?* (running) *Is he using his brain to run? Fill in the answer bubble for **yes** or **no**.* (yes) *Our brain tells our muscles to move.*

• *Point to box 4. Our brain is soft, gray, and wrinkly-looking. Can you see Noah's brain? Fill in the answer bubble for **yes** or **no**.* (no) *Why can't you see it?* (It's inside his head, protected by his skull.)

Day 2 activity

Life Science

• Understand that people are living things that have parts

Literacy

Oral Language Development

• Use new vocabulary

• Respond orally to simple questions

Comprehension

• Recall details

• Make connections using illustrations, prior knowledge, or real-life experiences

Developing the Concept

Distribute the Day 3 activity. Then introduce the activity by saying:

The brain is an important body part. It has many jobs. What are some of its jobs? (to help the body see, hear, touch, speak, move, learn, remember, breathe, etc.)

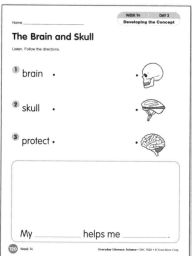

• *Point to the first word. It is **brain**. Let's read it together: **brain**. The brain tells our body what to do. Draw a line from the word **brain** to the picture of the brain.*

• *Point to the second word. It is **skull**. Let's read it together: **skull**. The brain is inside a hard bone called the skull. Draw a line from the word **skull** to the picture of the skull.*

Day 3 activity

• *Point to the third word. It is **protect**. Let's read it together: **protect**. Your skull protects your brain, so you need to protect your skull! Which picture shows something that can protect your skull?* (helmet) *Draw a line from the word **protect** to the picture of the helmet.*

• *Draw a picture of yourself in the box. Show something your brain helps you do. Then write the words to finish the sentence.*

Life Science
• Understand that people are living things that have parts

Literacy

Oral Language Development
• Respond orally to simple questions

Comprehension
• Recall details
• Make connections using illustrations, prior knowledge, or real-life experiences

Extending the Concept

Review that the brain is soft, gray, and wrinkly. Then say:

The brain is soft, so it is protected by the skull. But the brain may still get hurt in an accident.

> • *What can you do to protect your brain and skull?* (wear a helmet; be careful)

Distribute the Day 4 activity. Say:

• *These pictures show some ways the brain can be protected. Look at picture 1. What is the girl doing?* (playing baseball) *How does she protect her brain?* (wears a batting helmet) *Draw a star next to the girl.*

• *Point to number 2. What is the girl doing?* (riding in a car) *How does she protect her brain?* (wears a seat belt) *What does wearing a seat belt do?* (keeps her from hitting her head in an accident) *Color the seat belt straps.*

• *Point to number 3. What is the boy doing?* (riding his bike) *Is he protecting his head?* (no) *What did he forget to do?* (wear his bike helmet) *Draw a line from the bike helmet to the boy's head.*

• *Point to number 4. What is the girl doing?* (skating) *Is she protecting her brain?* (no) *What should she be wearing instead of a soft, floppy hat?* (a helmet) *Make an **X** on the girl's hat.*

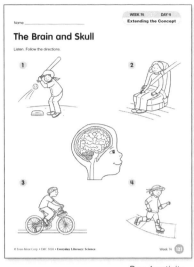

Day 4 activity

Hands-on Science Activity

Reinforce this week's science concept with the following hands-on activity:

Materials: a large open space, such as a playground

Background: This game is a variation of Simon Says, called "Your Brain Says."

Activity: Introduce the activity by saying:

This week we learned that the brain controls all the parts of the body. It tells our muscles when to move.

Let's play a game. If I say, "Your brain says jump up and down," you should jump up and down. If I say, "Your brain says shake your right hand," you should shake your right hand.

But if I say, "Hop on one foot," you must hold still because I left out the words "Your brain says."

Continue the game by giving movement instructions using the words "Your brain says," but occasionally leaving them out.

Name _____

The Brain and Skull

Name _____

The Brain and Skull

Listen. Fill in the circle for **yes** or **no**.

1. ○ yes   ○ no

2. ○ yes   ○ no

3. ○ yes   ○ no

4. ○ yes   ○ no

Name _____

The Brain and Skull

Listen. Follow the directions.

1 brain   •

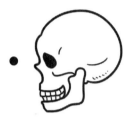

2 skull   •

3 protect •

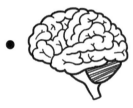

My _____ helps me _____.

Name _____

The Brain and Skull

Listen. Follow the directions.

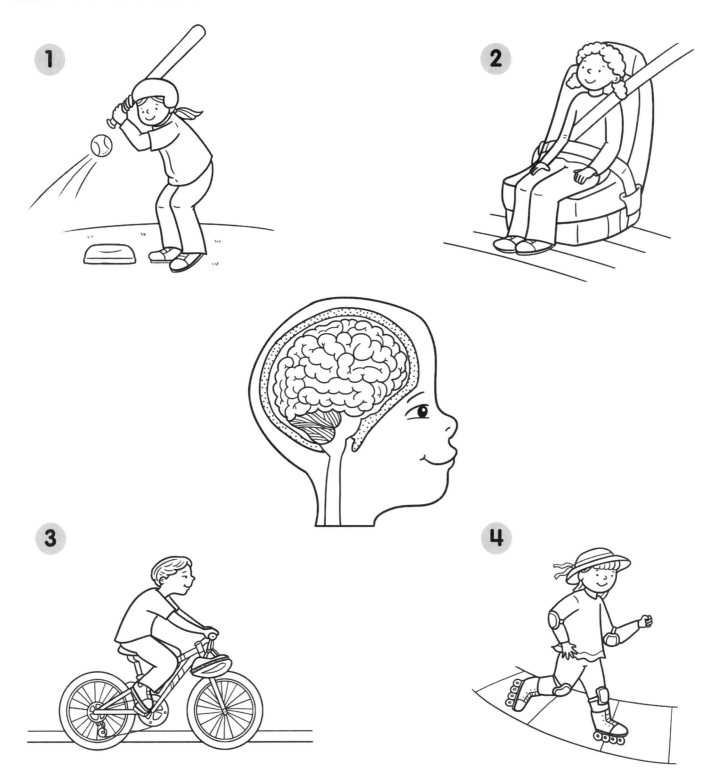

Name _____

What I Learned

What to Do
Have your child look at the pictures below and tell what each child
is doing. Then decide together which children are protecting their
brain and which are not.

WEEK 14

Home–School Connection

Science Concept: Living
things have parts.

To Parents
This week your child learned
about the functions of the
brain and skull.

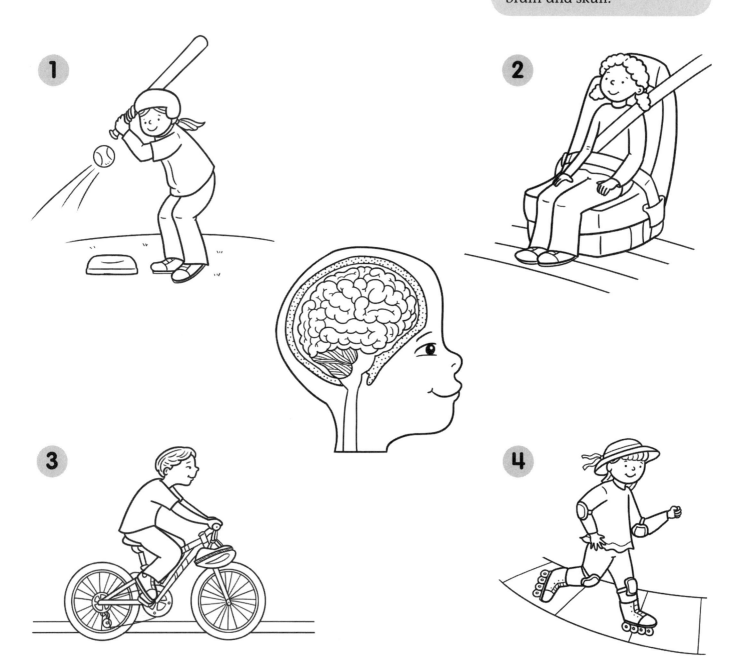

What to Do Next
Ask your child to name some ways in which the brain helps him or her at school.

Concept

Our bodies get energy from the foods we eat.

Food for Energy

Science Objective:
To help students learn how to choose from the five major food groups

Science Vocabulary:
beans, bread, cereal, dairy, fruit, grains, meat, milk, vegetable

Day 1
SKILLS

Life Science
- Understand that people, plants, and animals are living things with basic needs

Literacy

Oral Language Development
- Respond orally to simple questions

Comprehension
- Make connections using illustrations, prior knowledge, or real-life experiences
- Answer questions about key details in a text read aloud
- Make inferences and draw conclusions

Introducing the Concept

Bring in images or other props to represent the five food groups: **fruits**, **vegetables**, **meat** or **beans**, **grains**, and **dairy products**. Then say:

- *Your body gets energy from the foods you eat. You need energy to do all kinds of activities, such as running, playing, and going to school. To get the most energy, you should choose from the five food groups: fruits, vegetables, meat or beans, grains (which includes breads and cereals), and dairy (which includes milk and milk products, such as cheese and yogurt).*

- *What foods do you eat from these groups?* (students respond)

List students' suggestions in each of the categories.

Listening to the Story

Distribute the Day 1 activity page to each student. Say: *Listen and look at the picture as I read a story about a girl who makes good food choices.*

Marisa's family went to a restaurant to eat. They got in line and each took a plate. Marisa filled half her plate with fresh, colorful fruits and vegetables because they have lots of vitamins and minerals. She chose red grapes, a piece of bright yellow pineapple, some dark green broccoli, and a few orange carrots. For the other side of her plate, she helped herself to a piece of baked chicken and a whole-grain roll from a basket. Then, instead of a sugary soda, she chose fat-free milk to drink. It was a great power meal!

Confirming Understanding

Reinforce the science concept by asking questions about the story. Ask:

- *What kinds of fruit did Marisa choose?* (grapes, pineapple) *Circle the fruit.*

- *What kinds of vegetables did she choose?* (carrots, broccoli) *Color the broccoli green and the carrots orange.*

- *What kind of bread did she have?* (whole-grain roll) *Make a dot on the roll.*

- *What did Marisa drink?* (milk) *Why do you think she chose milk instead of soda?* (Milk is fat-free and has less sugar than soda.) *Draw a circle around the milk.*

Day 1 picture

Life Science

• Understand that people, plants, and animals are living things with basic needs

Literacy
Oral Language Development

• Respond orally to simple questions

Comprehension

• Recall details

• Make connections using illustrations, prior knowledge, or real-life experiences

• Make inferences and draw conclusions

Reinforcing the Concept

Reread the Day 1 story. Reinforce this week's science concept by discussing the story. Say:

Marisa filled her plate with foods from the five food groups. What are the five groups? (fruits, vegetables, meat/beans, grains, dairy)

Distribute the Day 2 activity. Say:

- *Point to box 1. To eat enough fruits and vegetables, we should fill half our plate with them. Did Marisa do that? Fill in the answer bubble for **yes** or **no**.* (yes)

- *Point to box 2. It's a good idea to choose fruits and vegetables in many colors. Did Marisa choose colorful fruits and vegetables? Fill in the answer bubble for **yes** or **no**.* (yes)

- *Point to box 3. The other half of our plate should have foods from the meat and grains groups. Marisa chose chicken and a whole-grain roll. Were they good choices? Fill in **yes** or **no**.* (yes)

- *Point to box 4. Does this picture show what Marisa chose for a drink? Fill in **yes** or **no**.* (no) *What did Marisa choose?* (milk)

Day 2 activity

Life Science

• Understand that people, plants, and animals are living things with basic needs

Literacy
Oral Language Development

• Respond orally to simple questions

• Use new vocabulary

Comprehension

• Make connections using illustrations, prior knowledge, or real-life experiences

• Make inferences and draw conclusions

Developing the Concept

To introduce the activity, say:

Food from the five groups gives us energy. It's important to eat the right amount of foods from each group. It's also important not to eat a lot of foods high in sugar or fat, such as cookies or fried foods.

Distribute the Day 3 activity. Say:

- *Point to number 1. This word is **fruit**. The pictures show apple pie and an apple. The pie is too sugary. Which one is a better choice to eat?* (fresh apple) *Circle the apple.*

- *Point to number 2. This word is **milk**. The pictures show soda and milk. The soda is sugary. Which one is better to drink?* (milk) *Circle the milk.*

- *Point to number 3. This word is **meat**. The pictures show a corn dog and a piece of roasted chicken. The corn dog is fried. Which one is better to eat?* (chicken) *Circle it.*

- *Point to number 4. This word is **bread**. The pictures show whole-grain bread and a doughnut. Which one is better to eat?* (whole-grain bread) *Circle it.*

- *Point to number 5. This word is **vegetable**. The pictures show raw carrots and french fries cooked in fat. Which one is better to eat?* (carrots) *Circle the carrots.*

Day 3 activity

Life Science

- Understand that people, plants, and animals are living things with basic needs

Literacy

Oral Language Development

- Respond orally to simple questions
- Use new vocabulary

Comprehension

- Make connections using illustrations, prior knowledge, or real-life experiences
- Make inferences and draw conclusions

Applying the Concept

Help students recall the Day 1 story. Say:

You should always fill your plate with healthful foods.

- *What two groups of food should be fresh and colorful?* (fruits and vegetables)
- *What are the other three groups you need?* (meat or beans, grains, dairy products)

Distribute the Day 4 activity. Say:

- *We are going to draw food on the plate to show what foods to eat for energy. Look at number 1. The word is **fruit**. What kind of food could you draw in this part of the plate?* (students respond) *Draw some fruit.*
- *Look at number 2. The word is **vegetables**. What kind of vegetables could you draw here?* (students respond) *Draw some vegetables.*
- *Look at number 3. The word is **grains**. What kind of bread or cereal could you draw in this part?* (students respond) *Draw some bread or cereal.*
- *Look at number 4. The words are **meat or beans**. What kind of meat or beans could you draw in this part of the plate?* (students respond) *Draw some meat or beans.*
- *Look at number 5. The word is **dairy**. What kind of milk product could you draw in this part?* (students respond) *Draw some milk or a milk product.*

Day 4 activity

Life Science

- Understand that people, plants, and animals are living things with basic needs

Scientific Thinking & Inquiry

- Sort objects according to common characteristics

Home–School Connection p. 130
Spanish version available (see p. 2)

Hands-on Science Activity

Reinforce this week's science concept with the following hands-on activity:

Materials: coffee filters, letter-size sheets of construction paper, scissors, glue, clip art of all five food groups

Preparation: Go to the website www.ChooseMyPlate.gov to download a picture of the five food groups arranged on a placemat. Print out the picture large enough to display.

Activity: Remind students that our bodies get energy from the foods we eat. Show students the My Plate picture, pointing out how the plate is divided into sections. Invite students to make their own plate on a placemat by flattening a coffee filter and gluing it onto the construction paper. Demonstrate how to divide the plate into four sections according to the My Plate picture. Then have students cut a smaller circle from another coffee filter for the dairy group. Finally, have students glue the food pictures in the corresponding sections. Laminate the placemats for students to use during mealtimes.

Name _____

Food for Energy

Everyday Literacy: Science • EMC 5026 • © Evan-Moor Corp.

Name _____

Food for Energy

Listen. Fill in the circle for **yes** or **no**.

Name _____

Food for Energy

Read the word. Circle the correct picture.

1 fruit

2 milk

3 meat

4 bread

5 vegetable

Everyday Literacy: Science • EMC 5026 • © Evan-Moor Corp.

Name _____

Food for Energy

Draw pictures for each food group. Then color your pictures.

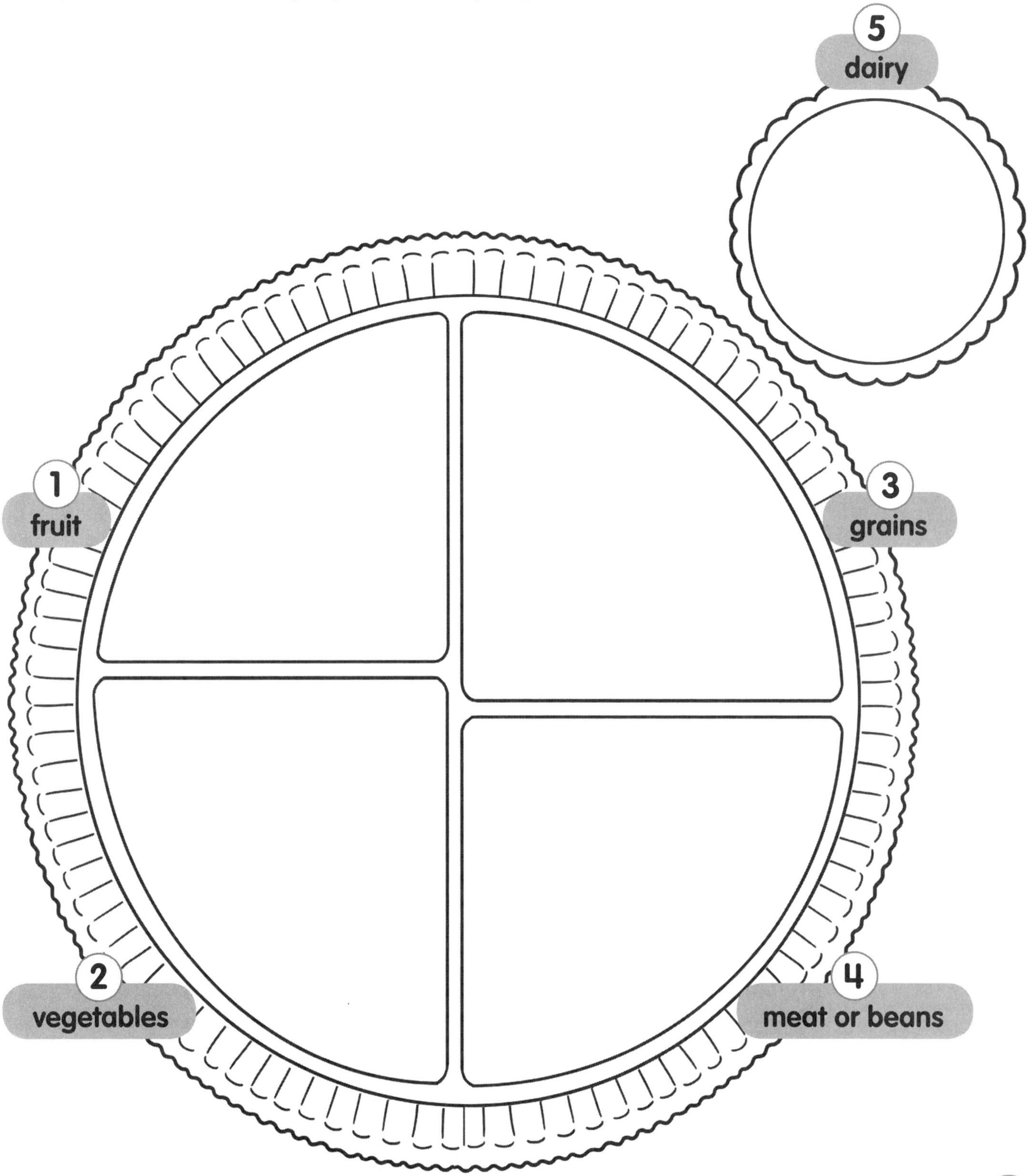

5
dairy

1
fruit

3
grains

2
vegetables

4
meat or beans

Name _____

What I Learned

What to Do
Have your child look at the picture below. Read each word to your child. Then ask your child to draw a food in each section that he or she eats. Talk about choosing low-fat or fat-free milk and milk products, along with whole-grain breads and cereals, for good health.

Science Concept: Our bodies get energy from the foods we eat.

To Parents
This week your child learned how to choose healthful foods that give him or her energy.

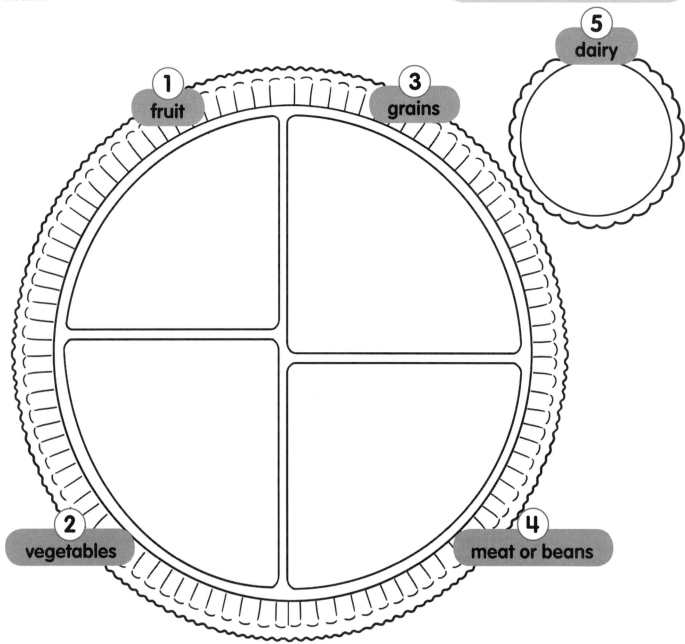

What to Do Next
Ask your child what new food he or she would like to try. Plan together to try a new fruit or vegetable this week.

Looking at Rocks

Science Objective:
To help students understand that rocks are changed by the weathering effects of wind, water, and ice

Science Vocabulary:
grains, ice, rock, sand, water, weathering, wind

Day 1
SKILLS

Earth Science
- Recognize that water, rocks, soil, and living organisms are found on Earth's surface
- Observe and describe differences in rocks

Literacy

Oral Language Development
- Respond orally to simple questions

Comprehension
- Make connections using illustrations, prior knowledge, or real-life experiences
- Answer questions about key details in a text read aloud
- Make inferences and draw conclusions

Introducing the Concept

Pass around several rocks for students to look at and touch. Say:

Rocks are very hard, but they can be changed. Wind, water, ice, and other forces cause rocks to fall, break, and become smooth. Big rocks become small rocks. Over many years, the small rocks get smaller and smoother until they become sand or soil. When natural forces such as wind, water, and ice change rocks, it's called **weathering**.

Listening to the Story

Direct students' attention to the Day 1 activity page. Say: *Listen and look at the picture as I read a story about Eric's day at the beach.*

Eric and his grandfather were walking along the beach. They came to a pile of rocks. Eric's grandfather pointed and said, "These rocks used to be a part of that cliff." At first, Eric was surprised. Then he watched the powerful waves crashing against the cliff. Eric could imagine how, over time, the water was wearing away the cliff and breaking off pieces of rock. That was why the top of the cliff stuck out like a shelf. "One day," said his grandfather, "that piece of cliff will come crashing down. And the rocks will break when they fall." Eric scooped up some sand and studied it. The tiny grains were the same color as the rocks. That's when he understood that the sand had been part of that cliff, too!

Confirming Understanding

Reinforce the science concept by asking questions about the story. Ask:

- *What did the waves do to the cliff?* (broke off pieces of rock) *Make an* **X** *on a wave.*

- *What will happen to the top of the cliff that is sticking out?* (It will fall down.) *Draw a line under the part that sticks out.*

- *What did Eric learn about the sand?* (It was once part of the cliff.) *Draw a line from the sand to the cliff.*

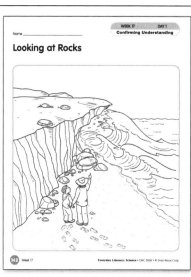

Day 1 picture

Day 2 SKILLS

Earth Science

• Recognize that water, rocks, soil, and living organisms are found on Earth's surface

Literacy

Oral Language Development

• Respond orally to simple questions

Comprehension

• Recall details

• Answer questions about key details in a text read aloud

Reinforcing the Concept

Reread the Day 1 story. Then reinforce this week's science concept by guiding a discussion about the story. Say:

Eric, the boy from our story, learns what water can do to rocks. What happened to the rocks that changed them? (They fell from the cliff and broke into pieces.)

Distribute the Day 2 activity. Say:

• *These pictures show **weathering**, or how wind and water changed a rock. Which picture shows what happened first?* (The wave crashed against the cliff.) *Draw a line from that picture to the number 1.*

• *Which picture shows what happened next?* (The rocks fell off the cliff.) *Draw a line from that picture to the number 2.*

• *Which picture shows what happened after that?* (The rocks broke into small pieces.) *Draw a line from that picture to the number 3.*

• *Which picture shows what happened last?* (The small rocks broke into even smaller pieces. They became sand.) *Draw a line from that picture to the number 4.*

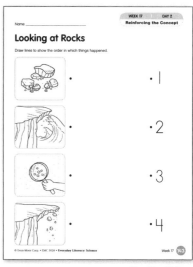

Day 2 activity

Day 3 SKILLS

Earth Science

• Recognize that water, rocks, soil, and living organisms are found on Earth's surface

Literacy

Oral Language Development

• Respond orally to simple questions

Comprehension

• Recall details

• Make connections using illustrations, prior knowledge, or real-life experiences

Extending the Concept

Introduce the activity by saying:

You learned that water causes weathering, or breaking down of rock. Wind also causes weathering. Wind carries small rocks. The small rocks hit larger rocks. The larger rocks break. They get smaller and smaller. After a long time, those small rocks become tiny grains of sand. Wind carries the sand everywhere, including the desert.

Distribute the Day 3 activity. Say:

• *Point to number 1. Weathering makes rocks smaller and smaller. Which of these rocks has been weathered by wind the most?* (small and round) *Draw a line under that rock.*

• *Point to number 2. What happens when small rocks hit larger rocks?* (The larger rocks get smaller.) *Next to the big rock, draw two smaller rocks.*

• *Point to number 3. How does sand end up in the desert?* (Wind carries the small grains of sand there.) *Color the wind that is blowing the sand.*

Day 3 activity

Earth Science

• Recognize that water, rocks, soil, and living organisms are found on Earth's surface

Literacy

Oral Language Development

• Use new vocabulary

• Respond orally to simple questions

Comprehension

• Make connections using illustrations, prior knowledge, or real-life experiences

Extending the Concept

Introduce the activity by saying:

Water and wind aren't the only things that cause weathering. Ice causes weathering, too. Water gets inside a crack in a rock. When water freezes into ice, it gets bigger, or expands. It can split the rock apart.

Distribute the Day 4 activity. Say:

Let's review some of the ways in which weathering can change rocks.

• *Point to the first word. Let's read it together: **water**. Water breaks down rocks into smaller pieces. Draw a line from the word **water** to the picture that shows water breaking down rock.*

• *Point to the second word. Let's read it together: **ice**. When it rains during very cold weather or snows, ice forms on and in rocks. When water freezes into ice, it expands. It breaks apart the rock. Draw a line from the word **ice** to the picture that shows ice breaking apart a rock.*

• *Point to the third word. Let's read it together: **wind**. Wind blows rocks off mountains. Wind also carries sand everywhere. Draw a line from the word **wind** to the picture that shows wind carrying sand.*

Day 4 activity

Earth Science

• Recognize that water, rocks, soil, and living organisms are found on Earth's surface

Scientific Thinking & Inquiry

• Gather and record information through simple observations and investigations

> **Home–School Connection p. 146**
> Spanish version available (see p. 2)

Hands-on Science Activity

Reinforce this week's science concept with the following hands-on activity:

Materials: ingredients to make "mock rock" dough (1 cup used coffee grounds, ½ cup cold coffee, 1 cup flour, ½ cup salt), sandpaper, water, one jar with lid for each student

Preparation: Mix the ingredients above to make the dough. Plan to have students work in groups of four. Prepare a batch of dough for each group.

Activity: Have each student form a mock rock out of the dough and let it dry overnight. The next day, invite students to simulate the effects of weathering on their rocks. For example:

• Have students rub sandpaper over their rocks to simulate wind blowing grains of sand against large rocks.

• Have students place their rocks in a jar of water and gently shake the jar.

• Encourage students to toss, rub, tumble, poke, and even drop their mock rocks. Then have each group of students discuss and record what happened to each of their rocks.

Name _____

Looking at Rocks

Name _____

Looking at Rocks

Draw lines to show the order in which things happened.

   •

• 1

   •

• 2

   •

• 3

   •

• 4

Name _____

Looking at Rocks

Listen. Follow the directions.

1

 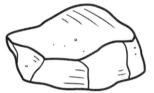

2

3

Name _____

Looking at Rocks

Listen. Draw a line from the word to the correct picture.

1 water •

2 ice •

3 wind •

Name _____

What I Learned

What to Do

Have your child look at the picture. Discuss how wind, water, ice, and other forces cause rocks to fall, break, and get smaller. Remind your child that this is called **weathering**. Ask your child to tell you how the water in the picture is weathering the rocks.

WEEK 17

Home–School Connection

Science Concept: Rocks are changed by natural forces.

To Parents

This week your child learned that water, wind, and ice change rocks.

What to Do Next

Take a walk with your child to look for signs of weathering on rocks. Look for small rocks broken off from bigger rocks, for example.

Bodies of Water

Science Objective:
To help students identify and describe a variety of natural bodies of water, including oceans, lakes, rivers, and streams

Science Vocabulary:
deep, flow, fresh, lake, narrow, ocean, river, salty, shallow, stream, water, wave, wide

Day 1
SKILLS

Earth Science
- Recognize that water, rocks, soil, and living organisms are found on Earth's surface
- Identify a variety of natural sources of water

Literacy

Oral Language Development
- Respond orally to simple questions

Comprehension
- Make connections using illustrations, prior knowledge, or real-life experiences
- Answer questions about key details in a text read aloud

Introducing the Concept

Display a globe and discuss what the colors represent. Say:

- *Most of Earth's water is in oceans. Have you ever been in an ocean?* (students respond) *An ocean is a large body of salt water.*

- *Have you ever been in a lake or river? Lakes are also bodies of water. They are smaller and are surrounded by land. Most have fresh water.*

- *Rivers and streams also have fresh water. They are bodies of water that flow, or move in one direction. A river is wide, but a stream is narrow.*

Listening to the Story

Distribute the Day 1 activity page. Say: *Listen and look at the pictures as I read a story about four cousins who live near water.*

---

*Once there were four cousins from different towns who all lived near water. Jake lived near an **ocean**. Its salty water was not good to drink, but the waves were fun to play in. Ana lived near a **lake**. She liked to sail on it. Her town got drinking water from the lake. David lived near a **river**. The water moved fast. It helped boats carry goods to other cities. Lisa also lived near moving water, but this body of water was smaller and moved more slowly than a river. Lisa lived near a **stream**, perfect for fishing. In the summer, the cousins visited each other and played in the water. They couldn't decide which was more fun: the ocean, the lake, the river, or the stream!*

Confirming Understanding

Reinforce the science concept by asking students questions about the story. Ask:

- *What is the largest body of water?* (ocean) *Why don't we drink ocean water?* (It's salty.) *Make an X on the ocean.*

- *What body of water is surrounded by land?* (lake) *Draw a circle around the lake.*

- *Which bodies of water are flowing?* (river and stream) *Draw a straight line down the river. Draw a wiggly line down the stream.*

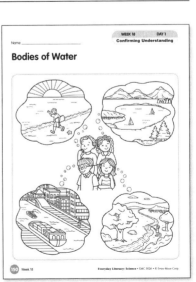

Day 1 picture

Day 2
SKILLS

Earth Science

• Recognize that water, rocks, soil, and living organisms are found on Earth's surface

• Identify a variety of natural sources of water

Literacy

Oral Language Development

• Respond orally to simple questions

Comprehension

• Recall details

• Make connections using illustrations, prior knowledge, or real-life experiences

Reinforcing the Concept

Reread the Day 1 story. Then reinforce this week's science concept by discussing the story. Say:

In our story, four cousins live near water.

> • *What is the large body of salt water called?* (ocean)

> • *What body of water is surrounded by land?* (lake)

> • *What two bodies of water flow?* (river and stream)

Distribute the Day 2 activity. Say:

> • *Point to box 1. An ocean is the largest body of water. Can we drink water from the ocean? Fill in the answer bubble for* **yes** *or* **no***.* (no) *Why not?* (It's salty.)

> • *Point to box 2. A lake is a body of water surrounded by land. Can people get drinking water from most lakes? Fill in the answer bubble for* **yes** *or* **no***.* (yes) *Yes, people can drink it if it is fresh water.*

> • *Point to box 3. A river is a long, wide, flowing body of water. Does water in a river move fast? Fill in the answer bubble for* **yes** *or* **no***.* (yes)

> • *Point to box 4. A stream is also a flowing body of water. Is it smaller than a river? Fill in the answer bubble for* **yes** *or* **no***.* (yes)

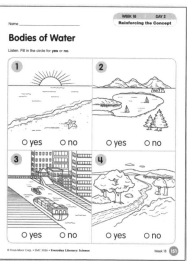

Day 2 activity

Day 3
SKILLS

Earth Science

• Recognize that water, rocks, soil, and living organisms are found on Earth's surface

• Identify a variety of natural sources of water

Literacy

Oral Language Development

• Respond orally to simple questions

• Use new vocabulary

Comprehension

• Make connections using illustrations, prior knowledge, or real-life experiences

• Make inferences and draw conclusions

Applying the Concept

Distribute the Day 3 activity. Then introduce the activity by saying:

I'm going to read some clues about bodies of water. Choose words from the word box to write the answer. Read the words with me: **river, lake, stream, ocean.**

> • *Point to box 1 and listen to the first clue: I contain most of Earth's water. I am salty. What am I?* (ocean) *Write the word* **ocean** *below the picture.*

> • *Second clue: I am surrounded by land. My water is usually not salty. What am I?* (lake) *Write the word* **lake** *below the picture.*

> • *Third clue: I am long and wide. I contain fast-moving water. What am I?* (river) *Write the word* **river** *below the picture.*

> • *Fourth clue: I am narrow and flowing. I am smaller than a river. What am I?* (stream) *Write the word* **stream** *below the picture.*

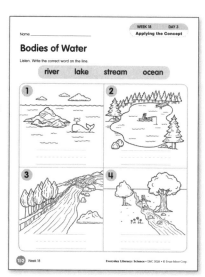

Day 3 activity

Earth Science

• Recognize that water, rocks, soil, and living organisms are found on Earth's surface

• Identify a variety of natural sources of water

Literacy

Oral Language Development

• Respond orally to simple questions

Comprehension

• Make connections using illustrations, prior knowledge, or real-life experiences

Extending the Concept

Introduce the activity by saying:

We have learned about oceans, lakes, rivers, and streams. They are different in many ways.

• *An ocean is **deep**. It is deeper than a lake.*

• *A river is usually deeper than a stream. A stream is **shallow**. In fact, the water may barely reach your knees!*

• *A river is **wide**. A stream is **narrow**.*

• *An ocean has **waves**. A lake may have waves, too. But a river and a stream do not have waves. They flow in one direction.*

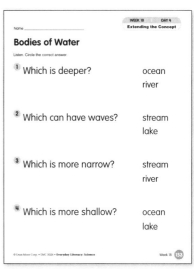

Day 4 activity

Distribute the Day 4 activity and say: *Let's answer some questions to compare bodies of water.*

• *Follow along as I read the first question: Which is deeper: an **ocean** or a **river**? Circle the answer.* (ocean)

• *Now follow along as I read the second question: Which can have waves: a **stream** or a **lake**? Circle the answer.* (lake)

• *Follow along as I read the third question: Which is more narrow: a **stream** or a **river**? Circle the answer.* (stream)

• *Follow along as I read the fourth question: Which is more shallow: an **ocean** or a **lake**? Circle the answer.* (lake)

Home–School Connection p. 154
Spanish version available (see p. 2)

Hands-on Science Activity

Reinforce this week's science concept with the following hands-on activity:

Materials: drawing paper, crayons or markers, pencils

Activity: Remind students of the bodies of water they have learned about: **ocean**, **lake**, **river**, **stream**. Brainstorm simple statements about each body of water, such as:

> *An ocean is big.*
>
> *A river flows.*
>
> *A stream is narrow.*
>
> *A lake has land around it.*

Record students' suggestions on the board or on chart paper. Read the sentences together. Have students choose one of the sentences to write at the bottom of the drawing paper. Then have them draw a picture to illustrate their sentence.

Name _____

Bodies of Water

Name _____

Bodies of Water

Listen. Fill in the circle for **yes** or **no**.

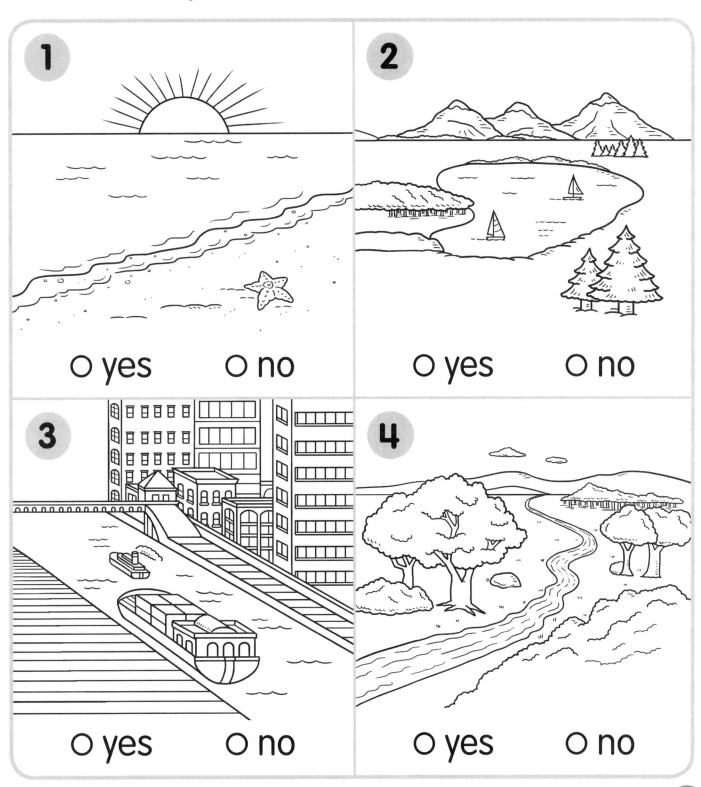

1
○ yes   ○ no

2
○ yes   ○ no

3
○ yes   ○ no

4
○ yes   ○ no

Name _____

Bodies of Water

Listen. Write the correct word on the line.

river   lake   stream   ocean

Everyday Literacy: Science • EMC 5026 • © Evan-Moor Corp.

Name _____

Bodies of Water

Listen. Circle the correct answer.

1 Which is deeper?   ocean

river

2 Which can have waves?   stream

lake

3 Which is more narrow?   stream

river

4 Which is more shallow?   ocean

lake

Name _____

What I Learned

What to Do
Have your child look at the pictures below, and read the words together. Ask your child to trace the words and match them to the pictures. Then have your child describe what distinguishes each body of water.

Science Concept: The Earth has rocks, soil, and water.

To Parents
This week your child learned to identify and describe natural sources of water: oceans, lakes, rivers, and streams.

1  •

2  •

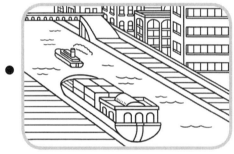

3  •

4 stream •

What to Do Next
Have your child describe fun water activities, such as swimming, boating, or fishing.
Ask what body of water he or she is envisioning.

Recording the Weather

Science Objective:
To help students understand that changes in weather can be observed, described, measured, and recorded

Science Vocabulary:
calendar, cloudy, measure, rain gauge, rainy, record, season, snowy, sunny, temperature, thermometer, weather vane, windy

Day 1
SKILLS

Earth Science
• Understand that weather can be observed and measured using simple tools
• Understand that weather changes across days and seasons

Literacy

Oral Language Development
• Respond orally to simple questions

Comprehension
• Recall details
• Make connections using illustrations, prior knowledge, or real-life experiences
• Answer questions about key details in a text read aloud

Introducing the Concept

Introduce the concept by activating students' knowledge about weather. Say:

• *Weather changes from season to season and day to day. What is the weather like today?* (students respond) *What is the weather like in the winter? spring? summer? fall?* (students respond)

Then display a thermometer or a picture of one and say:

• *We use tools to measure weather. One tool is a* **thermometer**. *It measures temperature, or how hot or cold something is. The liquid in a thermometer goes down when the temperature gets colder. It goes up when the temperature gets warmer. The numbers tell us what the temperature is.*

Listening to the Story

Distribute the Day 1 activity page to each student. Say: *Listen and look at the picture as I read a story about a girl who is recording the weather.*

Riley is recording how the weather changes from day to day and season to season. She writes the temperature and weather symbols on her calendar every day. First, she goes outside to feel the temperature of the air. Then she looks at the thermometer. It says 80 degrees. Riley writes the temperature on the calendar. She holds her hand out and feels a warm wind blowing. She looks up at the flag and sees it waving back and forth. She draws the symbol for wind on her calendar. Finally, she looks up at the sky and sees the sun shining. She draws the symbol for sun on the calendar. Riley goes inside to tell her mom that the weather is sunny and windy and the temperature is 80 degrees. It is a perfect summer day!

Confirming Understanding

Reinforce the science concept by asking questions about the story. Ask:

• *What does Riley write on the calendar to record the weather?* (temperature and weather symbols) *Circle a weather symbol on the calendar.*

• *What measures the temperature of the air?* (thermometer) *Circle it.*

• *Look at Riley's calendar. Did the weather change from day to day?* (yes) *Make an* **X** *on the coldest day.*

Day 1 picture

Earth Science

• Understand that weather can be observed and measured using simple tools

• Understand that weather changes across days and seasons

Literacy

Oral Language Development

• Respond orally to simple questions

Comprehension

• Answer questions about key details in a text read aloud

• Make inferences and draw conclusions

Reinforcing the Concept

Reread the Day 1 story. Then reinforce this week's science concept by guiding a discussion about the weather. Say:

Weather changes across days and seasons. What was the weather like yesterday? (students respond) How is the weather the same or different today? (students respond)

Distribute the Day 2 activity and markers. Say:

• *Point to picture 1. What can you tell me about the weather in this picture? (It is hot and sunny.) Write a weather symbol in the box to record the weather.*

• *Point to picture 2. Tell me about the weather in this picture. (It is cloudy and rainy.) Write two weather symbols in the boxes to record the weather.*

• *Point to picture 3. Look at the weather symbol and the thermometer. Draw a picture that shows someone outside in that kind of weather.*

• *Point to picture 4. The liquid in a thermometer goes down as the temperature gets colder. What happens to the liquid when the temperature gets warmer? (it goes up) With a marker, fill in the thermometer to show a warmer temperature. Then draw a picture of yourself on a warm day.*

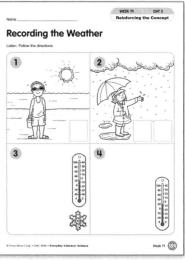

Day 2 activity

Earth Science

• Understand that weather can be observed and measured using simple tools

• Understand that weather changes across days and seasons

Literacy

Oral Language Development

• Use new vocabulary

Comprehension

• Make connections using illustrations, prior knowledge, or real-life experiences

Applying the Concept

To introduce the activity, guide a discussion that reviews different types of weather. Ask:

What words can we use to describe the weather? (sunny, cloudy, rainy, windy, snowy)

Distribute the Day 3 activity. Say:

• *Point to the chart. It has a symbol and a word each day to show the weather. Let's read the words together: **Monday, windy; Tuesday, sunny; Wednesday, cloudy; Thursday, rainy; Friday, snowy.***

• *Now point to sentence 1. It says **Monday was _____**. Look at Monday on the chart. What was the weather? (windy) Write the word **windy** in the boxes to finish the sentence.*

After students finish writing, say:

*Now let's read the sentence together: **Monday was windy.***

Repeat the process for the remaining days.

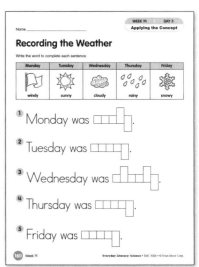

Day 3 activity

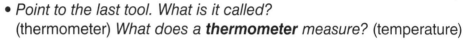

Day 4
SKILLS

Earth Science

- Understand that weather can be observed and measured using simple tools
- Understand that weather changes across days and seasons

Literacy

Oral Language Development

- Respond orally to simple questions

Comprehension

- Make connections using illustrations, prior knowledge, or real-life experiences
- Make inferences and draw conclusions

Extending the Concept

Distribute the Day 4 activity and say:

We use tools to observe and measure weather. Look at the tools at the top of the page.

- *The first tool is called a **weather vane**, or a **wind vane**. Have you ever seen a weather vane on top of a building? (students respond) A weather vane shows which direction the wind is blowing: north, south, east, or west.*

- *The next tool is called a **rain gauge**. It measures how much rain has fallen.*

- *Point to the last tool. What is it called? (thermometer) What does a **thermometer** measure? (temperature)*

- *Point to picture 1. The weather is cold and rainy. We want to know how much rain fell. Which tool can we use? (rain gauge) Draw a line from the picture to the rain gauge. How many inches of rain has this rain gauge measured? (2 inches)*

- *Point to picture 2. It's a really cold day. It's snowing! What tool will tell us exactly how cold it is? (thermometer) Draw a line to the thermometer. How cold is it in degrees Fahrenheit? (20 degrees)*

- *Point to picture 3. Not only is it cold, but it's windy, too! What tool will tell us in which direction the wind is blowing? (weather vane) Draw a line to the weather vane. Draw wind swirling around the weather vane.*

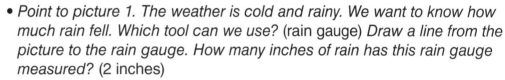

Day 4 activity

Day 5
SKILLS

Earth Science

- Understand that weather can be observed and measured using simple tools

Scientific Thinking & Inquiry

- Gather and record information through simple observations and investigations
- Interpret information found in charts

Home–School Connection p. 162
Spanish version available (see p. 2)

Hands-on Science Activity

Reinforce this week's science concept with the following hands-on activity:

Materials: chart paper, marker, outdoor thermometer

Preparation: Draw a chart that shows Monday through Friday. Designate an area on the chart to write the name of the month and season. Decide what time (or times) of day your class will record the temperature.

Activity: Record the month, the season, and the daily changes in weather. Model how to read the thermometer. Place it outdoors and read it at the same time each day. Write the temperature on the chart and discuss the temperature changes. At the end of the week, discuss the chart. Ask:

- *Was any day cold (or hot) this week? Is this normal weather for this season? What did you probably wear that day?*

- *Which day was the warmest this week? Which was coldest or coolest?*

To extend the activity, go online each day to compare the temperature at school with the temperature in two other cities familiar to students, for example, Mexico City and Des Moines, Iowa.

Name _____

Recording the Weather

Everyday Literacy: Science • EMC 5026 • © Evan-Moor Corp.

Name _____

Recording the Weather

Listen. Follow the directions.

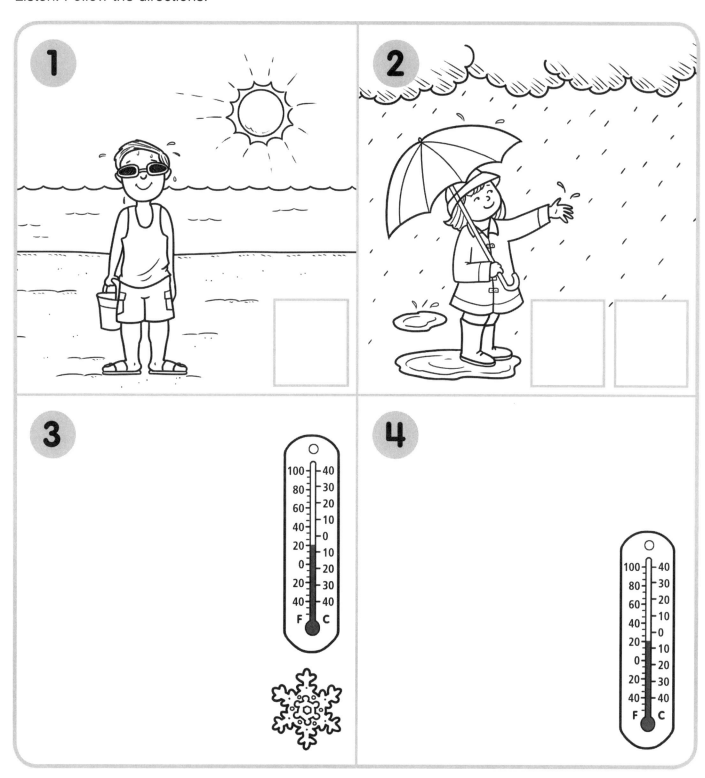

Recording the Weather

Write the word to complete each sentence.

Monday	Tuesday	Wednesday	Thursday	Friday
windy	sunny	cloudy	rainy	snowy

1 Monday was ⬜⬜⬜⬜⬜.

2 Tuesday was ⬜⬜⬜⬜⬜.

3 Wednesday was ⬜⬜⬜⬜⬜⬜.

4 Thursday was ⬜⬜⬜⬜⬜.

5 Friday was ⬜⬜⬜⬜⬜.

Name _____

Recording the Weather

Listen. Follow the directions.

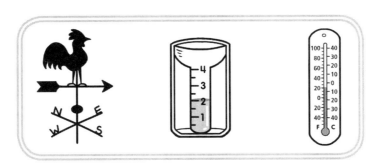

1

2

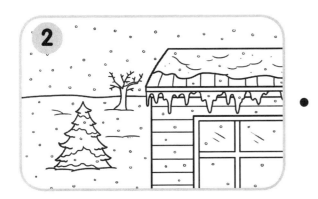

3

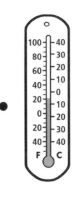

Name _____

What I Learned

What to Do
Have your child use the chart below to record the weather he or she observes for five days. Ask your child to look at the weather symbols. Then have him or her draw a symbol representing the weather each day. If an outdoor thermometer is available, have your child record the temperature as well.

Science Concept:
Weather changes across seasons and from day to day.

To Parents
This week your child learned that weather changes from season to season and from day to day.

My Weather Chart

Monday	Tuesday	Wednesday	Thursday	Friday

What to Do Next
Help your child use a computer with an Internet connection to compare the weather and/or temperature where you live with the weather in another city, perhaps where a friend or a relative lives.

Our Sun

Concept

People, plants, and animals need the sun's heat and light.

Science Objective:
To help students understand why the sun is necessary for life on Earth

Science Vocabulary:
cold, heat, hot, light, plants, ray, star, sun, warm, warmth

Day 1 SKILLS

Earth Science
- Understand that the sun supplies heat and light and is necessary for life

Literacy

Oral Language Development
- Respond orally to simple questions

Comprehension
- Recall details
- Make connections using illustrations, prior knowledge, or real-life experiences
- Answer questions about key details in a text read aloud

Introducing the Concept

Introduce the concept that the sun is necessary for life on Earth. Say:

- *The sun is a burning star millions of miles away. It is so hot that its heat and light reach us on Earth. The sun warms the land, air, and water. Do you feel its warmth more during the day or at night?* (students respond)

- *Sunlight makes plants grow. Without the sun, there would be no plants. People and animals need plants for food.*

Listening to the Story

Distribute the Day 1 activity page. Say: *Listen and look at the picture as I read a story about how the sun helps people and plants.*

One sunny day, Dad invited Mason to the garden. "It's a beautiful day! Come out and get some sun!" he said. Mason stepped out into the bright sunlight. The warm rays felt good on his face. "Can you imagine Earth without the sun? It would be cold and dark all the time," said Dad. "We couldn't live in a place like that. No plants would grow. People need plants for food and other things. So do animals." Mason bent over to check a tomato plant. It was full of ripe red tomatoes and healthy leaves. He popped a small tomato into his mouth. It was warm from the sun, and it was delicious. Mason was grateful for the sun that warms the Earth and helps plants grow.

Confirming Understanding

Reinforce the science concept by asking students questions about the story. Ask:

- *What would Earth be like without the sun?* (cold and dark) *Make a yellow dot on the sun.*

- *How does Mason feel about the sun?* (He likes the warm rays on his face.) *Draw a line from the sun to Mason's face.*

- *Is the sun important to plants?* (yes) *Are plants important to people?* (yes) *Why?* (They give food and other things.) *Make a green **X** on a tomato plant.*

Day 1 picture

Earth Science

• Understand that the sun supplies heat and light and is necessary for life

Literacy

Oral Language Development

• Respond orally to simple questions

Comprehension

• Recall details

• Make connections using illustrations, prior knowledge, or real-life experiences

• Answer questions about key details in a text read aloud

• Make inferences and draw conclusions

Reinforcing the Concept

Reread the Day 1 story. Then reinforce the science concept by discussing the story. Say:

Our story was about why we need the sun.

- *Does the sun provide heat and light to the Earth?* (yes)

- *Why do plants need the sun?* (Heat and light help them grow.)

Distribute the Day 2 activity. Say:

- *Point to box 1. What does the picture show?* (watering can) *The sun helps living things grow and live. Does the watering can need the sun? Fill in the answer bubble for* **yes** *or* **no**. (no)

- *Point to box 2. The sun helps plants grow. Is the sun helping these plants grow? Fill in the answer bubble for* **yes** *or* **no**. (yes) *How do you know?* (They look healthy; Tomatoes are growing.)

- *Point to box 3. Plants make food for animals. Does this animal eat plants? Fill in the answer bubble for* **yes** *or* **no**. (yes) *What foods do people get from cows?* (milk, meat)

- *Point to box 4. Without the sun, Earth would be cold and dark. No plants or animals could live here. Does this picture show Earth without the sun? Fill in the answer bubble for* **yes** *or* **no**. (no)

Day 2 activity

Earth Science

• Understand that the sun supplies heat and light and is necessary for life

Literacy

Oral Language Development

• Respond orally to simple questions

• Use new vocabulary

Comprehension

• Make connections using illustrations, prior knowledge, or real-life experiences

Applying the Concept

Introduce the activity by reviewing the science concept. Say:

The sun is very important to us on Earth. Without the sun, we could not live here.

Distribute the Day 3 activity. Say:

- *We are going to write words to finish these incomplete sentences. Point to the first word in the gray box. Let's read the words together:* **sun**, **live**, **warm**.

- *Now point to sentence 1. Read it with me:* **The sun keeps me _____.** *Write the word that completes the sentence.* (warm) After students write the word, read the sentence together.

- *Point to sentence 2. Read it with me:* **Plants need the _____.** *Write the word that completes the sentence.* (sun) After students write the word, read the sentence together.

Continue the process with sentence 3. Then say: *Look at the box at the bottom of the page. Draw a picture of something that needs the sun.*

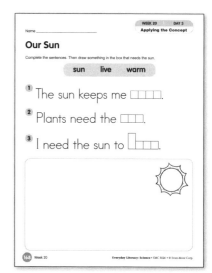

Day 3 activity

Earth Science

• Understand that the sun supplies heat and light and is necessary for life

Literacy

Oral Language Development

• Respond orally to simple questions

Comprehension

• Make connections using illustrations, prior knowledge, or real-life experiences

Applying the Concept

Distribute the Day 4 activity and crayons. Then introduce the activity by saying:

Look at the picture. Many things in this picture need the sun in order to live and grow. Draw a sun in the picture. Then make a dot on each thing that needs sunlight. Put your crayon down when you are finished.

Allow students time to complete the activity. After they are finished, say:

Day 4 activity

• *Let's talk about the things you made a dot on. Did you make a dot on the flowers?* (yes) *Why?* (Plants need sunlight to grow.)

• *Did you mark the girl?* (yes) *Why?* (People need sunlight for warmth. People eat plants.)

• *Did you make a dot on the chicken?* (yes) *Why?* (Animals need sunlight, because they eat plants.)

• *Did you make a dot on the toys?* (no) *Why?* (Toys are not alive and don't need sunlight.)

• *Now color the things that you made a dot on.*

Earth Science

• Understand that the sun supplies heat and light and is necessary for life

Scientific Thinking & Inquiry

• Gather and record information through simple observations and investigations

> **Home–School Connection p. 170**
> Spanish version available (see p. 2)

Hands-on Science Activity

Reinforce this week's science concept with the following hands-on activity:

Materials: three rocks of the same type

Preparation: On letter-size paper, create a 3-column "heat chart" with the column headings **Cold, Warm, Hot.** Reproduce the chart, one for each pair of students. Set out numbered rocks in different areas: 1) shaded area indoors; 2) shaded area outdoors; 3) sunny area, etc.

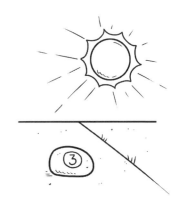

Activity: Distribute the chart to each pair of students. Assign partners the roles of tester and recorder. The tester feels each rock and gauges its warmth relative to the other rocks. Which rock is cold? warm? hot? The recorder writes the rock's number on the chart. Stimulate awareness of the sun's widespread warming effects. Say:

• *The sun warms the land, and rocks are part of the land. Which rock was hottest to the touch? Why do you think that was? Which rock was coolest to the touch?* (students respond)

• *The sun warms the air. Where did the air feel warmer to you, in the sun or in the shade?* (students respond)

• *The sun warms the water. What if we did this experiment with pans of water? Do you predict similar results?* (students respond)

Name _____

Our Sun

Name _____

Our Sun

Listen. Fill in the circle for **yes** or **no**.

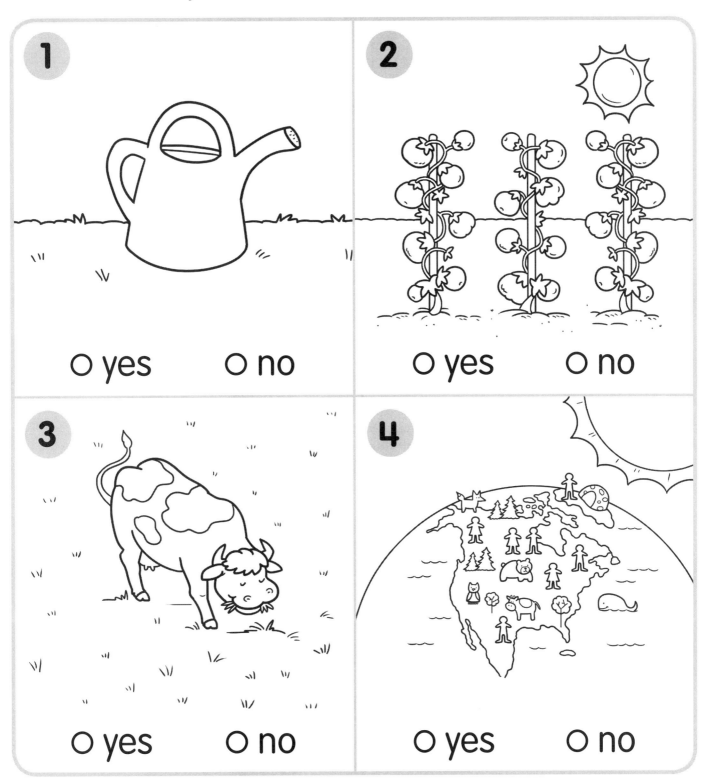

1
○ yes   ○ no

2
○ yes   ○ no

3
○ yes   ○ no

4
○ yes   ○ no

Name _____

Our Sun

Complete the sentences. Then draw something in the box that needs the sun.

| sun | live | warm |

1 The sun keeps me ⬜⬜⬜⬜.

2 Plants need the ⬜⬜⬜.

3 I need the sun to ⬜⬜⬜⬜.

Name _____

Our Sun

Listen. Color the things that need the sun to live and grow.

Name _____

What I Learned

What to Do
Have your child tell you which things in the picture need the
sun in order to live and grow. (plants, animals, people) Then
have your child color the picture.

Science Concept: People,
plants, and animals need the
sun's heat and light.

To Parents
This week your child learned
that the sun is necessary for life
on Earth.

What to Do Next
Get two identical potted plants. Leave one plant in a shady spot and the other on a sunny
windowsill. Have your child observe which plant looks healthier after two weeks and ask him
or her to explain why.

Answer Key

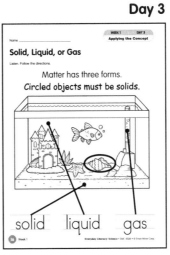

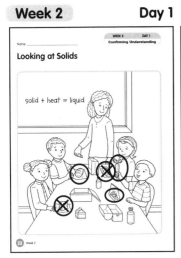

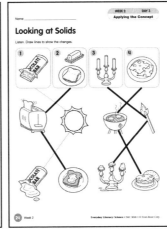
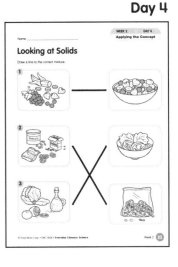

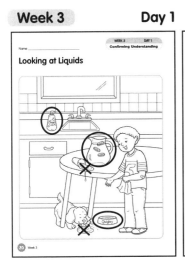

Week 4

Day 1

Day 2
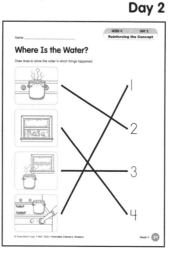

Day 3

Day 4
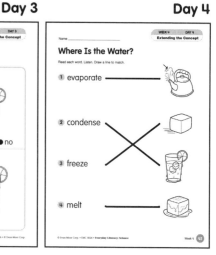

Week 5

Day 1
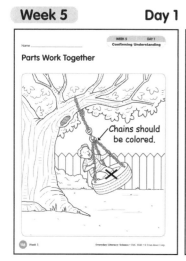

Day 2
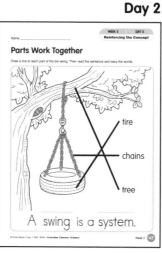

Day 3
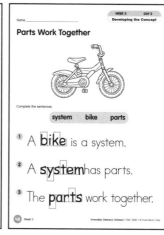

Day 4
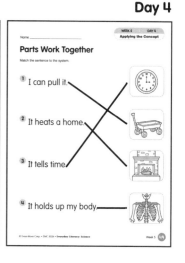

Week 6

Day 1

Day 2

Day 3
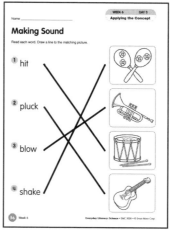

Day 4
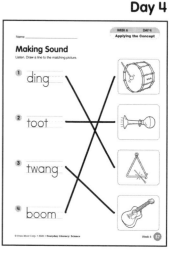

Week 7

Day 1

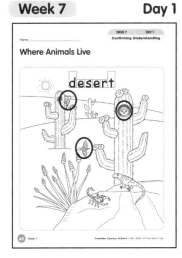

Day 2

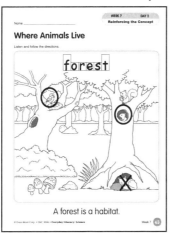

Day 3

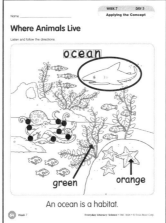

Day 4

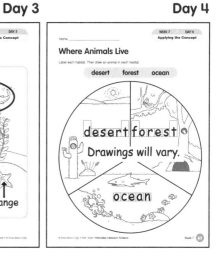

Week 8

Day 1

Day 2

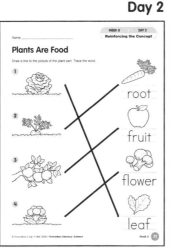

Day 3

Day 4

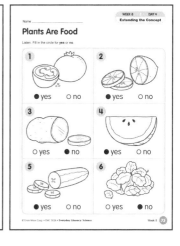

Week 9

Day 1

Day 2

Day 3

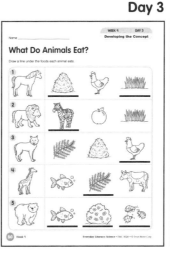

Day 4

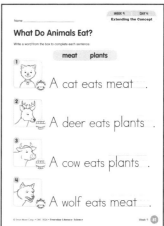

Week 10

Day 1

Day 2

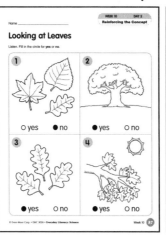

Day 3

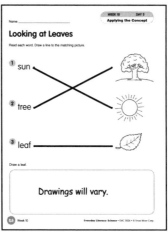

Day 4

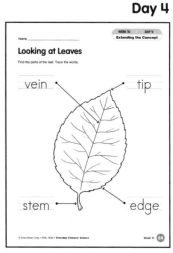

Week 11

Day 1

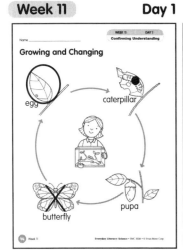

Day 2

Day 3

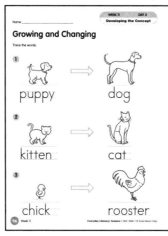

Day 4

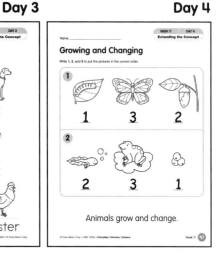

Week 12

Day 1

Day 2

Day 3

Day 4

Week 13

Day 1

Animals and Their Babies

Day 2

Animals and Their Babies

Listen. Fill in the circle for **yes** or **no**.

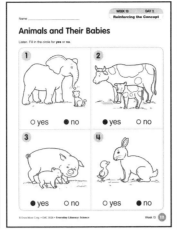

1. ○ yes ● no
2. ● yes ○ no
3. ● yes ○ no
4. ○ yes ● no

Day 3

Animals and Their Babies

Read and trace. Then draw a line to the correct picture.

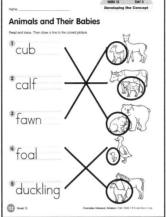

1. cub
2. calf
3. fawn
4. foal
5. duckling

Day 4

Animals and Their Babies

Write the baby's name. Then circle the animal it becomes.

kid   cub   piglet   chick

1. kid — goat, deer, horse
2. chick — duck, pig, chicken
3. cub — bear, rabbit, squirrel
4. piglet — cow, goat, pig

Week 14

Day 1

The Brain and Skull

Day 2

The Brain and Skull

Listen. Fill in the circle for **yes** or **no**.

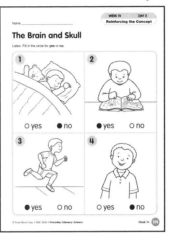

1. ○ yes ● no
2. ● yes ○ no
3. ● yes ○ no
4. ○ yes ● no

Day 3

The Brain and Skull

Listen. Follow the directions.

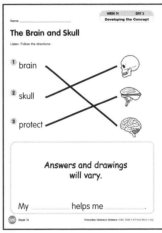

1. brain
2. skull
3. protect

Answers and drawings will vary.

My _____ helps me _____

Day 4

The Brain and Skull

Listen. Follow the directions.

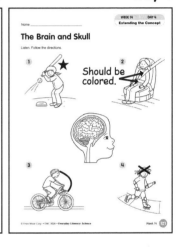

Should be colored.

Week 15

Day 1

Food for Energy

green   orange

Day 2

Food for Energy

Listen. Fill in the circle for **yes** or **no**.

1. ● yes ○ no
2. ● yes ○ no
3. ● yes ○ no
4. ○ yes ● no

Day 3

Food for Energy

Read the word. Circle the correct picture.

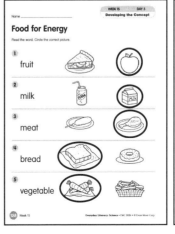

1. fruit
2. milk
3. meat
4. bread
5. vegetable

Day 4

Food for Energy

Draw pictures for each food group. Then color your pictures.

Drawings will vary, but should correspond to each group.

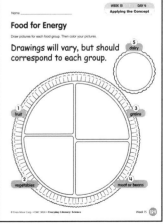

1. fruit
2. vegetables
3. grains
4. meat or beans
5. dairy

Parts of an Insect

Back legs should be colored.

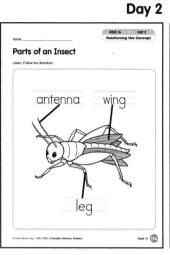

Parts of an Insect

Listen. Follow the directions.

antenna   wing

leg

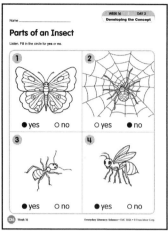

Parts of an Insect

Listen. Fill in the circle for **yes** or **no**.

1. ● yes   ○ no
2. ○ yes   ● no
3. ● yes   ○ no
4. ● yes   ○ no

Parts of an Insect

Color the insects.

The butterfly, grasshopper, and bee should be colored.

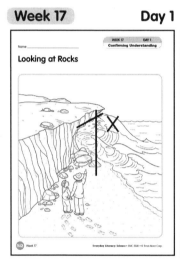

Looking at Rocks

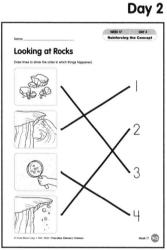

Looking at Rocks

Draw lines to show the order in which things happened.

1
2
3
4

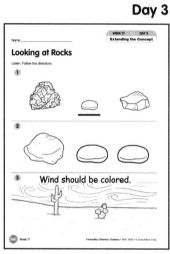

Looking at Rocks

Listen. Follow the directions.

1
2
3. Wind should be colored.

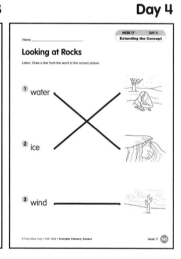

Looking at Rocks

Listen. Draw a line from the word to the correct picture.

1. water
2. ice
3. wind

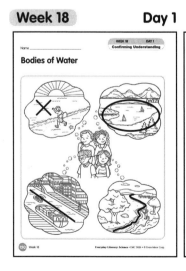

Bodies of Water

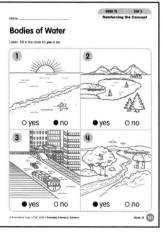

Bodies of Water

Listen. Fill in the circle for **yes** or **no**.

1. ○ yes   ● no
2. ● yes   ○ no
3. ● yes   ○ no
4. ● yes   ○ no

Bodies of Water

Listen. Write the correct word on the line.

river   lake   stream   ocean

1. ocean
2. lake
3. river
4. stream

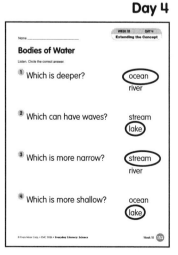

Bodies of Water

Listen. Circle the correct answer.

1. Which is deeper?   (ocean)   river
2. Which can have waves?   stream   (lake)
3. Which is more narrow?   (stream)   river
4. Which is more shallow?   ocean   (lake)